THE LEGEND OF THUNDAR

THE LEGEND OF THUNDAR

Ed March

iUniverse, Inc.
Bloomington

The Legend Of Thundar

iUniverse books may be ordered through booksellers or by contacting:

iUniverse
1663 Liberty Drive
Bloomington, IN 47403
www.iuniverse.com
1-800-Authors (1-800-288-4677)

ISBN: 978-1-4620-4567-9 (sc)
ISBN: 978-1-4620-4570-9 (hc)
ISBN: 978-1-4620-4568-6 (ebk)

Printed in the United States of America

iUniverse rev. date: 08/02/2011

For Keys, with love.

Prologue

Zirac the sorcerer stared down on Empire City. Despite his vantage point from the highest window in the tallest tower at Royal Castle, the trivial creations of man, the streets and boulevards and the dwellings of innumerable shapes and sizes, spread farther into the distance than he could see. Contempt welled up in his heart in a wave so strong he could nearly taste it on his tongue: the peasant class of humanity had ruled the Empire for far too long. Change was coming.

A waif floated into the the room, the pathetic creature only a disembodied eyeball in physical form, bobbing through the air as if riding a river of other-dimensional currents.

"A woman approaches," came its telepathic message.

"Escort her here."

Zirac waited impatiently. Booted feet clomped on the flagstones. A woman approached with the waif. The woman wisely kept her distance from the child of darkness.

Zirac stifled a smirk: the woman's appearance resembled a collision between a street harlot and an actress playing the role of a military commander, as she was adorned equally with feminine attire and a man's tools of war. The daggers slung low off her hips and a light sword in a scabbard strapped to her back looked ridiculous combined with a tunic so scanty that any self-respecting woman would have been embarrassed to reveal even half so much bare skin in public. A pair of jack boots covered her bare legs to the knees. Brown hair hung reaching nearly to the floor, tresses that might prove acceptable material for a broom. He forced a smile to his lips.

"Katja, good to see you."

The woman smiled stupidly under his praise.

"What do you want, sorcerer?"

"Why, only to have a little talk, Katja. To see how you are doing, and perhaps to discuss a little business beneficial to us both."

"Business? You? Planning to open up a bathhouse?" She laughed stupidly.

"Hardly that kind of business. How are you doing these days, Katja?"

"Skip it, Zirac, you've never cared about how anybody is doing in your life. All you care about is your power."

"Unlike you."

"I have my eyes set on profit, not power." She tapped her foot. "You asked me to come to this little secret meeting of yours, so out with it. What do you want?"

"I want what's best for everybody," Zirac said. "Didn't you know? I've always desired what is best for the Empire and its subjects. My heart is pure."

"You're wasting my time." She turned as if to leave.

"In short, should the Emperor continue with his present set of policies, the Empire will suffer."

"The Empire?" She smirked. "A certain magician will lose his seat on the royal counsel. The Emperor has made his intentions clear on that much at least."

Zirac shook his head. "I'm but a single man and hardly am in a position to create mischief even if I were so inclined, which I'm not. Persecuted is what magicians are, abused as a people. Penned up like a herd of cattle at Wizardhome. It's a disgrace."

"You should be telling this to the Emperor, not to me."

"His plans are also said to include doing away with all mercenary companies throughout the Empire, and to declare the personal possession of weapons illegal, excepting of course for those in the hands of soldiers and the police. An unarmed populace."

"That's just a rumor." The woman's voice rose a pitch. "You don't know the Emperor's plans. You're just speculating. And if what you say is true, then that's bad news for everybody, not just us mercenaries."

"I don't know?" Zirac forced another smile to his lips. The muscles in his face twitched from the unfamiliar exercise. "My dear, I sit on the counsel on a daily basis. Trust me, I know."

She scoffed. "Trust you."

"What if there was a way so that these destructive policies never became law?"

The woman's voice dropped low. "What do you mean? Your spells and such leave marks on their victims, everybody knows that."

"Do not think I am so crude as to cast a spell on any living person. I certainly would not have summoned you to my presence if such were my plan."

"I wasn't summoned." The woman held up a gold coin. "You passed me a note wrapped around this."

"Did you examine the image on that piece?"

Katja held the coin close to her face. "What about it?"

"Do you not recognize the profile of your beloved King Dexter? While the tragedy of the Crazy Wars is admittedly a long time back in the past . . . ."

"Where did you get it?"

"The answer to that question is privileged, but rest assured, there's plenty more where that coin came from. Five-hundred more pieces in fact, all of which I'm willing to depart with for certain services from your troupe."

The woman tensed even as her voice remained nonchalant. Her hand slid down to her hip. "Do you have the loot with you now?"

"Are you about to attack me?" Zirac said. "The waif would be on you in an instant. Its touch would blast your soul and freeze your blood. And I have defenses of my own that you can only dream of. Get your hand off that dagger and listen to me."

"What?" She smirked again. "Attack the most powerful wizard in the land? Are you out of your mind? You're growing paranoid in your old age, Zirac."

He attempted another smile, but his face positively ached.

"You're not growing any younger either, Katja, so listen up . . . ."

Chapter One

Prince Gerald of North Bogsonia maneuvered his small boat between a pair of overgrown lilly pads. The push pole in his hands sank deep into the muddy bottom with each stroke.

The afternoon sun blazed down like a hammer through the cloudless sky. Steam rose from the water, forming sheets of rainbow-colored mist. Atop the rare patches of high ground, purple life-siphon trees clustered in carnivorous masses, their meaty feeding vines dangling down from stout branches with a seeming casualness. Razor grass and black tulips lifted clear of the water in great jumbles. Parasitic needle weed and sucker thistle vied for space among stands of grass. Insects swarmed overhead. Dragonflies fluttered among the reeds on wingspans as wide as a man's outstretched arms. Birds of every conceivable size and type and color chirped and sang and darted through the air. A riot of growth.

An alligator slid into the water from atop a log and paddled alongside the boat for a moment, moving ever nearer, but just as Gerald was about to lay down his pole in favor of a bow, the reptile slunk away through the thick cover of vegetation and disappeared. A prickling sensation against the back of his hand drew his attention, and he flicked away a jumping leech before the slimy parasite had a chance to get its jaws set firmly into his skin.

A clacking sound erupted from among the tall grass just ahead, a hollow beat delivered at the pace of a frantic drum roll. Heart pounding, he exchanged the push pole for his bow. The grass rustled. The clacking noise grew louder. He notched an arrow and drew the bowstring all the way back to his cheek.

A swamp beetle emerged from the grass, a fully grown male judging by its size, armed with massive pincher jaws, an exoskeleton harder than steel, and lightning-quick reflexes. Gerald estimated this specimen to weigh around five-hundred pounds.

"Over here," he taunted.

The beetle rattled another challenge and reared back up on its hind legs. Gerald let loose the bowstring. The speeding arrow struck the beast in the center of its unprotected underside, sinking deep. A clear ichor jetted from the wound. The beetle toppled over on its back. Tiny, underdeveloped wings beat the ground furiously. Compound eyes glazed over. A noxious stench filled the air.

"A successful hunt," called a voice from behind.

Gerald glanced back over his shoulder.

"Better not miss the target when faced off with a swamp pincher. Why do you bother me when I am on the hunt, Rogan?"

"My apologies." The grizzled warrior's coat of chain mail rustled as he poled his boat closer. "But our wise king requests your presence at court."

"What for?"

Rogan shrugged. "I was instructed to seek out your royal self and advise you of the king's orders. It was hardly my place to demand further explanations." He indicated the carcass with an outstretched finger. "Were you tracking this thing?"

Gerald nodded. "There were reports that people were being waylaid. I was in the mood for some exercise, so I tracked it down myself."

Rogan let out a low whistle. "It's been eating pretty well as of late. It's huge."

Gerald smiled. "Cut down on tourism is what it's bound to do. North Bogsonia needs all the outside currency we can get our hands on."

"Tourism? You saw a tourist?"

"A couple of seasons back, remember? Those folks from down south."

"That party of ogres? They were lost. They died from swamp fever."

"Not them, the two researchers from Empire City." Gerald worked his push pole in the water, backing away from kill.

"How could I be so stupid? Of course I remember. Hey, what about your beetle? It's a trophy."

"It's all yours." Gerald tried to avoid breathing through his nose. "What a stink."

Leaving the carcass where it lay, they poled the boats westward and approached the royal road, a narrow strip of exposed bedrock that cut a meandering path through the entirety of North Bogsonia, and the sole means of overland travel for hundreds of miles in any direction. Cypress trees towered beside the shoulders of the road, massive specimens reaching upwards of two-hundred feet or more, each branch and leaf providing precious shade against the searing sun.

Gerald dragged his boat atop the shoulder of the road and flipped the vessel over. Leeches fell to the ground by the dozen as he scraped the push pole against the wet hull.

"I wonder what my father wants me to do? It can't be good."

Rogan beat the parasites from his boat as he spoke.

"I wasn't informed, but rest assured, if an idea comes from the mind of King Gerald V, you know it'll be brilliant."

Gerald laughed. "I'll mention to him that you said that."

Rogan grinned. "I'd appreciate it."

They left the boats at the edge of the water and set out at a brisk walk down the road, keeping to the shade whenever possible. A wooden bridge spanned a gap in the road, one of several artificial walkways leading back to the castle. Guttural speech broke out from beneath the bridge almost as soon as their boots rattled off the slatted deck.

"Are those goblins I hear up there?" said a thick voice. "Smells like goblins."

"Are you goblins headed for Bogwood?" called another. "You're going the wrong way. You must have gotten turned around. You're going to get lost."

"Sad," Rogan said.

Gerald glanced over the railing and spotted a family of trolls sprawled on the ground near the edge of the water below, a pungent smell giving away their presence even had they chosen to remain quiet, which trolls almost never did.

"They're nothing but a nuisance," he said. "It'd be nice if they could learn to curb their breeding habits, but I suppose that I might as well wish the sky a different shade of blue."

"Maybe they're ogres," called a troll. "Sound as dumb as ogres. Dumber."

"Unfortunately," Gerald continued, "both the breeding and the insulting are in their nature."

"Shouldn't let them in North Bogsonia, not if that's how it's going to be," Rogan muttered. "Not that I'm critical of any of the king's policies, far from it. The man is brilliant."

Bogwood rose high above the surrounding countryside. The mesa upon which the capital city of North Bogsonia was situated could only be reached by a single road, a narrow and steep path easily defended and nearly impossible for attackers to use to their own advantage. Stone walls fifty feet high interrupted by guard towers surrounded the massive, central castle keep. Giant granite blocks lent extraordinary strength to the walls. The entire site sparkled under a white limestone finish that on a sunny day hurt a man's eyes to gaze directly upon. As if in a tribute to the preceding decades of peace, hundreds of small personal dwellings were scattered outside the confines of the walls, entirely unprotected in the event of an attack.

Gerald felt a stirring of pride at the sight of the heavy portcullis at the main gates. The massive iron doors were capable of dropping shut in an instant if the city came under attack. When the inevitable happened, and the trolls and ogres and goblins chose to once more rise up and make war on mankind, as they had so many times before in the past, Bogwood Castle would be ready. He hoped.

A troupe of fawning servants stood at the entrance to the palace.

"Prince Gerald, we were so worried," simpered a young woman.

"Thank the stars you're safe," said her male counterpart. "The gods be praised."

Gerald walked through the doorway without comment, crossed the foyer in a few steps, and entered the throne room without waiting to be announced. Rogan followed close behind.

King Gerald V sat unsteadily atop a golden throne. A crown perched crookedly atop his head. Red-tinged eyes stared out from beneath bushy eyebrows. Grog blossoms marred his face. A massive slab of stomach grotesquely extended his royal waistline. Behind the throne stood a host of slaves, consultants, advisors, and fawners, a small army primed for the chance to perform some errand for their liege and thereby win his approval. Seated in lesser chairs on either side of the throne were Gerald's elder brothers, Rupert and Herod, busily slurping at their cups.

"Where have you been?" King Gerald said.

"Hunting in the gardens."

"You were still outside? I'd have thought the sun would have driven you indoors hours ago. I can't stand the heat like I used to."

Gerald smiled to show that he understood. "What was the nature of the emergency requiring my immediate presence?"

"Big news." The king motioned with his hand.

Prince Gerald leaned near the throne.

"We received a report from our mole in South Bogsonia today," King Gerald said. "It appears that the old degenerate himself, Maurice the Weak, has sent an envoy to Empire City bearing gifts for the Emperor's birthday. North Bogsonia must respond in kind. As a united people."

"As a united people," Gerald repeated.

A young servant trod up to the throne bearing a platter loaded with swamp kabobs, deep fried crawfish, pickled fish eyes, and other delicacies. The King motioned for the oversized dish to be placed directly upon his lap and proceeded to gorge. Twice he choked, coughing for a spell as if about to asphyxiate, but in the end the food disappeared without serious mishap. A tremendous belch echoed through the throne room. The platter was whisked away.

"That's right," the King said. "United as a people. While the Emperor is admittedly a close personal friend of mine, what good to tie the the the glory of our nation to one man, to myself alone?"

Prince Gerald ventured a guess. "No good?"

"Terrible is more like it," the King said. "You will therefore travel to Empire City and act as our emissary on the occasion of the Emperor's seventy-fifth birthday. That degenerate, Maurice, sent his third born son. We must not be outdone by those hillbillies."

"Wouldn't the kingdom be better served sending one of my brothers instead of my lowly self? Surely someone closer to inheriting the throne would impress the Emperor that much more."

Rupert and Herod frowned simultaneously.

"No," King Gerald said. "Maurice has set the precedent, and so I must respond in kind."

Rogan the Axe Slayer stepped forward. "Let me be the first to volunteer for Prince Gerald's party."

The King squinted. "Rogan, yes of course, you are a brave man. But be warned: I traveled to the Empire once in my youth. Empire City is a hell unfathomable, and barely habitable by human standards."

"That bad?" Rogan frowned. "But scores of people live out that way, or so they say."

"That much is true," King Gerald admitted. "Though why they choose to live in such a place is beyond my imagining. The entire western lands are so dry as to be nearly devoid of life. Many miles separate one lake or river from the next. Air without a trace of moisture. It leaves your skin wrinkled like parchment in no time."

Rogan tilted back his chin. "I care not about the risk, nor the hardships."

"I care," Gerald said.

"The journey is treacherous, there's no other way to describe it." King Gerald shrugged. "But these concerns matter not. The greater issue here is that the Emperor must not lose sight of what loyal and valuable vassals he possesses in North Bogsonia."

"How could he forget us?" Gerald said. "We are the Empire's first line of defense against invasion."

"Why the frown, boy?" King Gerald took a long drink from his mug. "Think I don't understand? Leave the beauty of god's country for a wasteland? Can't say as I blame you for being reluctant, but the gods have dictated that on occasion a man must challenge himself, to rise above his wants and lusts and personal hungers and do what needs to be done. This is just such an occasion—for you. Truth of it is that when I was your age, I had no interest in sitting around on a throne. I had to force myself to do it. I still do. All I really desire is a chance for carousing and adventure, but the responsibilities as king have proven too burdensome." He held up his mug. "More wine."

"You made the Empire sound just awful," Rupert said. "No wonder he doesn't want to go."

"Sounds dirty," Herod agreed.

"I will appoint a team to accompany you on the journey to Empire City," King Gerald said.

"I volunteer to be a member of that team, Sire," Rogan called out.

"Yes, yes, I heard you the first time." The King pursed his lips. "A mission of such vital importance requires the presence of a full team of assistants, starting with a chronicler to record all that happens for posterity. Our old friend, Puppet, would be the best choice."

"Perhaps two or three generations ago he would have been the best choice," Gerald said. "But Puppet is now too old and feeble to walk the length of the palace floor without assistance, let alone travel all the way to Empire City and back again."

"He's over a hundred seasons old," the King said. "What do you expect? But yes, perhaps his assistant, Parrot . . . ."

Gerald frowned. "I don't know the man personally. Is he of strong personal character?"

The King waved his hand. "Who cares? Seeing as there's only a few among us who can make sense of the squiggly lines on parchments, our choices are somewhat limited."

"I could seek to remember all that we see and do," Rogan suggested. "Then I could repeat it all to a chronicler once we get back."

The King nodded. "You see, boy? There's your choice, Parrot's ink quill or Rogan's memory."

"I'll go with Rogan's memory," Gerald said.

"That was a rhetorical question, you're taking Parrot with you. A chronicler will be of invaluable assistance deciphering road signs or public notices you might pass on your journey. It's best if he go along."

Gerald managed to keep from scowling.

"Now that I think of it," the King said, "you'll need a full honor guard, not just some bare bones crew. This is the Emperor's birthday we're talking about. There'll be no end to the pomp and ceremony in Empire City."

Gerald scowled deeply. "A long and dangerous journey is best undertaken with a small party. A large group is less efficient to move around by far."

King Gerald shook his head. "Efficiency takes a secondary consideration in these situations, what with the glory of North Bogsonia at stake and all. Come, you're usually all in favor of any sort of adventure, but now you're looking positively glum. Is it the evil ones?"

Gerald shrugged.

King Gerald waved his hand. "Worry not about the wizards. The fiends are kept under careful watch at Wizardhome, as they have been ever since the end of the Crazy Wars. Only a single mage is allowed in the Emperor's court, and he will never notice your presence or stoop so low as to speak to a mere mortal such as yourself anyway. Only if the mage takes an interest in you, then you'll know for certain there's foul play afoot." He laughed uproariously.

Gerald shuddered. "At least that last part is reassuring."

Chapter Two

Pug the castle servant reached the spy hole in the darkness of the utility corridor just as two nobles entered Zirac's personal chambers.

"We can talk freely here," one noble said. He barred shut the door.

The speaker's brown robes were embossed with images of dragons and lions in golden thread. His fingers twinkled with gems.

The plainer garb of the other man contrasted with the garishness of the first.

"This room has been checked for spies?" said the second man.

"Zirac cast a spell in here earlier today. Our words can't travel beyond the center of the room."

"Good. Saves me the need to cut anyone's throat."

Pug fought down a surge of fear: standing rules forbade castle guests from visiting injury upon the Emperor's servants, but the powerful and mighty were an unpredictable lot, driven by fear and prone to violent outbursts. He remained very, very still.

The man in plain robes sat down on a chair. "The individuals that you and your master requested shall arrive tonight. They have travelled far."

"I requested no one," said the other noble, still smiling. "My client requires certain rare items. From where those goods originate and the people delivering them is irrelevant. But this is good news indeed, for now it can begin."

"I will advise you the moment they arrive."

"I scarcely need to remind you that above all else, neither of us can be seen in the company of those men, not under any circumstances. My name must not be associated with them in any way, nor yours. Councilor Lewis's people are sure to demand a full investigation afterward, and we mustn't provide the authorities an excuse to come slavering in our direction."

Pug slid his feet backward, shuffling one soft-soled shoe behind the other. The voices faded in the distance. His shaking hands grew steady.

The maintenance passages and service ways used by the Emperor's servants to remain out of the sight of castle guests led past countless air grates, hidden alcoves, and even the occasional bedroom. Listening in on the guests was regarded as a serious crime by palace officials, and grounds for instant dismissal among other punishments, but the temptation of spying on important people was a temptation all but impossible to resist. Alliances agreed upon and broken. Extramarital affairs. Murder. Betrayal of all kinds. As surely as the sun rose in the morning, nobles worked ceaselessly to gain the upper hand over their fellow kind, and no act was too foul in the promotion of that end.

These particular nobles Pug classified as both more wary and more reckless than most, cautious enough to seek out a private spot for their meeting but foolhardy to rely on a mage for their personal security. The ineffectiveness of Zirac's spell piqued Pug's interest. The voices of the plotters carried clearly to his hiding spot. Could it be possible that Zirac was in fact not as powerful in the dark arts as generally assumed?

No. The Wastelands and the Blastedlands stood as irrefutable proof of the powers available to sorcerers when their collective backs were up against a wall. Entire rivers turned to dust. Forests petrified. Previously fertile countryside scorched to lifeless barrens. That the leader of the sorcerer's guild wielded strength enough to cast a spell of silence in a small room seemed beyond doubt. Perhaps Zirac had double crossed his co-conspirators, pulled some trickery that involved guaranteeing their anonymity but all the while left them exposed to betrayal? For what gain? The twists and turns left him shaking his head.

"Boo."

Pug jumped at the sound of the unexpected voice. His heart pounded against his chest.

"Scared you." Jonas, servant second class, tittered like a school girl. "Where have you been?"

"Quiet," Pug whispered. "Go back. I'm right behind you."

He shoved Jonas to prod the boy into action.

They made their way down the corridor and continued through a smaller passageway, emerging at last at a trapdoor at the back of a kitchen pantry. The cooking area bustled with cooks and assistant cooks and servants of all kinds. The evening meal approached.

"What's your hurry?" Jonas complained.

"I almost stumbled over a couple of nobles in a meeting and didn't want to be accused of spying. You know how it is."

Jonas's eyes went wide. "They might have become angry if you had been seen."

"They might have stabbed me, given a chance." Pug shook his head. "You should have heard them. Some workers or craftsmen or some such are about to arrive in Empire City, and these nobles want to keep their arrival quiet, probably to avoid paying some entitlement or other."

"They sound like typical nobles."

Pug scratched his head. "They sounded more vicious than usual, that's all. I suppose I shouldn't be too surprised considering they were discussing their first love, that being money."

"You there!" A scowling kitchen cook waved her wooden spoon in the air. "You two, back there in the pantry. Hiding even as the master's meal is about to be served. For shame. Go out back and fetch some firewood for the oven right now. And there had better not be any more slacking going on."

Pug hurried to carry out the old woman's instructions before her spoon transformed into a bludgeon. Jonas scampered along at his side.

Chapter Three

Gerald watched from the side of the street as the royal column moved out through the main gates of Bogwood. A contingent of a dozen soldiers, hard looking men in gray chain mail, led the parade. A quartet of drummers in sparkling red uniforms followed. Flag bearers walking along opposite sides of the road held aloft the crimson banner of North Bogsonia. Cooks, assistant cooks, servants, porters, and others brought up the rear.

"I see that my father in his infinite wisdom decided to send half the royal court."

Porters hauled immense packs upon their backs and simultaneously directed oaken wine barrels down the road with their sandaled feet. A select team carried a palanquin bearing the Emperor's birthday gift. A wrap of purple cloth covered the precious cargo. Court performers and cloth menders shuffled along with the rest.

"Fifty-four individuals by my count," Rogan said. "A large group to take all the way to Empire City. The mountain passes will test them sorely."

Gerald clenched his teeth. "How long before the first one comes up lame? It's almost enough to make me understand why folks in other lands ride atop horses."

"I think I heard somewhere that the early settlers of North Bogsonia kept dozens of the beasts," Rogan said. "Or that they tried to."

Gerald nodded. "I can just imagine that scene. Between diseases, drownings, bad water, alligators, swamp beetles, and all the rest, those pioneers would have needed to replace the entire stable every few days."

"Personally, I think it's the main reason why North Bogsonia received a reputation as a hard and wild place. The southerners are weak. Even their animals are weak."

"They do seem to be unable to deal with the lushness of the land," Gerald said.

Rogan shrugged. "It's their loss. Besides, now North Bogsonia has a healthy population."

"Ten thousand isn't such a vast number of people," Gerald said. "Not by the Empire's standards. Empire City alone has many times more."

"I only claimed that we have a healthy population, not that we're teeming in numbers like leeches. What would be good about that? Life would be crowded if there were so many folks living in one place."

Parrot trotted up to Gerald's side. The royal chronicler's youthful face shone with naive exuberance.

"Speaking of those who will likely slow us down . . . ," Rogan said.

Parrot smiled. "My friends, please excuse the interruption, but did I just hear a soldier talking history? Perhaps I can be of assistance?"

"We were discussing the early days of North Bogsonia," Gerald said. "In particular, the fate of the early pioneers "

Parrot nodded vigorously. "Mean you those traitors that fled the Emperor's troops for siding with the ogres, goblins, and magicians during the Crazy Wars?"

"I prefer to refer to them as pioneers," Gerald said. "What do you know of the era?"

Parrot shrugged. "Most of the criminals, I mean, most of the early pioneers died soon after their arrival."

"Horses," Rogan said. "We were discussing the fate of the beasts they rode."

"The horses all died, of course," said the chronicler. "As did any farm animals they might have brought with them, be it cattle, sheep, or goats. The were yet to learn that only those born to the swamp can survive here."

The tail end of the travel party approached the portcullis.

"I trust you will be accurate in your descriptions of our expedition, chronicler," Rogan said. "It's been my experience that soldiers are oftentimes maligned in the official record by scholarly types. Portrayed as men of violence rather than enforcers of peace. Slandered by peaceniks."

"Accuracy is a given for a royal chronicler," Parrot said. "Accuracy above all, that's our motto. On that note, how many axes have you slain, Rogan the Axe Slayer? I must ask for the sake of the record."

"Are you daft?" Rogan said. "Men call me Axe Slayer because I defeat enemies with my axe, not because I kill axes. An axe isn't even alive, it's just a piece of iron. How would you kill it?" He turned to Gerald. "This whelp is charged with keeping track of our doings for the sake of official Bogsonian history? He doesn't even understand basic stuff."

"You miss my point," Parrot said. "Would Joe the Deer Hunter defeat an enemy using a fresh kill? Would he swing a carcass about like a club or some such? Of course not. The honorarium of a deer hunter is bestowed upon an individual who hunts and kills deer, not one who uses a slab of venison to smite his foes. Logically speaking then, an axe slayer . . . ."

"My name inspires fear." Rogan's face darkened. "And you had better remember that in the record, if you know what I'm saying."

Parrot scrawled on a small piece of parchment. "With that threatening attitude, you just might go down in history as having worn a woman's dress, if you know what I'm saying."

"Now listen you little—"

"No more of that," Gerald said. "Parrot, you keep an accurate account of all that transpires, regardless of whether you like Rogan's title or any other for that matter, and Rogan, you are forbidden from slaying Parrot no matter how bothersome his company."

Parrot opened his mouth as if to object.

"And that's the end of it." Gerald set off after the travel party.

The last house before the city walls was a nondescript structure, a whitewashed single family bungalow, unremarkable in every way except that as Gerald passed by, the front door swung open and a rotund woman stepped out. Her face was twisted in a scowl, and her close set eyes squinted to mere slits. Deep wrinkles spiraled from the edges of her mouth to cheekbones as if in memory of a lifetime of frowning.

"What are you up to this time, Rogan?" she hollered.

Rogan hunched his shoulders and accelerated to a brisk walk.

"Where do you think you're going?" the woman shrieked. "I have chores for you to do. You'd better not be running off on some fool's errand. Tell the king you're needed at home and get back here right now."

Rogan broke into a trot. He sped through the portcullis.

"Get back here!" The woman shouted a succession of profanities.

"Dare I ask the identity of that wonderful person?" Parrot said.

Gerald smiled. "Rogan's wife, of course. Why do you think he was in a rush to join this party? Because he's brave?"

Parrot smiled. "He didn't even inform his own spouse that he was leaving Bogwood? That won't look very good in the official chronicles. I'll have to make sure to mention it to him."

The woman barked a final curse and retreated back within the house, slamming the door with a terrific crash.

"Not that I blame Rogan," Parrot said. "I wonder why he doesn't simply divorce her?"

Gerald ignored the comment.

"I think I might know," Parrot said. "Perhaps it's because divorce is still illegal in North Bogsonia. Talk about backward. Tragic that a noble warrior like Rogan the Axe Slayer can only find peace by fleeing his home simply because his sweet young bride grew up to become an old shrew."

"Tragic," Gerald said.

Parrot sniffed. "An injustice that you would have the opportunity to right were you ever to gain the throne."

Gerald laughed. "Don't bother lobbying me. I'll never get within ten feet of the throne."

The royal column made nearly twelve miles that first day before Gerald ordered a halt for the night. Cook fires supplied heat for food preparation as well as the smoke necessary to drive back the clouds of flying insects. Gerald tore into his meal of grilled swamp boar, boiled cattail root, and deep fried juicy critters with unreserved gusto. A side dish of smoked bass set his taste buds alive. A mug of wine took the edge off his thirst.

Parrot pulled up a stool and sat down along the opposite side of the fire. Rogan showed up with a couple of his men, Red and Skunk. Conversation was muted. The last rays of the setting sun basked the land in a ruby glow. Gerald's eyes grew heavy.

"Dragonbat approaching," called a guard.

Gerald sprang to his feet.

As black as night, a dragonbat bore down on their position riding a thirty-foot wingspan. Curved talons hung down from the barrel-shaped body like twin clusters of scimitars. The squished face resembled a ghoul straight out of a child's nightmare. Fangs glistened whitely despite the failing light.

"Archer," called Gerald.

A bowman strode up to his side.

"Put a bolt beside that thing and see if it frightens off."

The dragonbat let loose a hair-raising screech, a call from a more primordial era, ancient and evil. Servants and cooks and porters dropped to the ground.

The bowman let loose an arrow. The shaft passed beside the triangular head without noticeable effect.

"Put one though its wing," Gerald ordered.

The second arrow tore through the bat's left wing without slowing, leaving behind a fist-sized hole in the membrane. The bat wavered in the air like a sickly bird, still screeching but now in an entirely different tone. It veered away from the road in a shallow bank.

"Why not kill it?" Rogan demanded. "Dangerous beast."

"Dangerous mainly to gators and unwary trolls," Gerald said. "Good pest control otherwise. The troll problem would likely be even worse than it is without them. Maybe this one will recover and learn to be more wary of the scent of man but still live to eat many trolls. Let it escape."

The archer put down his weapon.

The stricken bat flew back in the direction from which it came and disappeared over the horizon.

"That's the first real big one I've seen all summer," Rogan said. "Though not for want of their natural food. Trolls are about as common as leeches these days."

"The dragonbat are said to be nearly extinct," Parrot claimed. "When the rock giants fled their human pursuers following the end of the Crazy Wars, they overran the caves and crags that were the dragonbat's main breeding grounds. The bats have dwindled in number ever since. It'd be sad in a sense if we just mortally wounded one of the last ones. Almost like killing the last unicorn, though admittedly, it was about to attack us."

Gerald smiled. "No need to record that particular event in the official history. You saw what happened. I could just as easily have ordered that arrow planted in its chest when it came in on us like that."

Parrot scratched his head. "You instructed me to accurately record everything that happens on this journey. You stressed the accuracy part."

"Everything within reason," Gerald said. "It goes without saying that a man in your position needs to practice some discretion."

"I see," Parrot said. "Keep an accurate account of all that happens, but within reason, and remembering to practice discretion."

"Exactly." Gerald returned to his stool and sat. "Common sense I call it."

"Would common sense dictate the inclusion of an itinerary of our trip in the official history?"

Gerald nodded. "Sure. Seeing as how the north pass remains blocked by the rock giants, we have no choice but to travel southward along the Blasted Lands until we reach the town of Speck. There we will charter a ship to Bandit, and then onward through the Great Southern Pass, across the lands of Plenty, and we'll practically be in Empire City. Nothing to it, though I think we'll skip the side trip to Wizardhome."

Rogan spat. "Not safe having a den of wizards anywhere in the Empire. Look what happened. The army should have exterminated the fiends when they had the chance."

"They tried." Gerald shrugged. "But times have changed. The Crazy Wars will never be repeated, not so long as the wizards are all kept in one place."

"Better now with the peace enforced by half sober men with swords and axes," Parrot said. "Can't get enough of that type."

"Right on," Rogan said. "Most intelligent thing you've said all day."

Gerald glanced around the camp. "We'll need to charter a fairly large boat to transport all these people across Lake Unpleasant."

"An ark is more like it," Parrot said.

Gerald frowned. "Let the record show that I recommended we travel as lightly as possible, but that court etiquette trumped common sense, or so my father insisted. We might need to charter two smaller vessels if nothing large enough is available."

"Perhaps a fleet," Parrot said.

"Now don't you go and start exaggerating in the History," Gerald warned. "We don't want to look foolish. Common sense, remember. And truth."

"Of course." Parrot scratched at a parchment. "I should have thought to check through the old histories before we left regarding the size of the party when your father last made this trip."

"My father was a child when he journeyed to Empire City. It's likely he doesn't remember the event very clearly."

"It seems likely that he didn't remember it at all." Rogan shook his head. "Some of these people already look the worse for the wear. A couple of them were limping before we stopped today. And it's only been one day."

"Not to worry," Gerald said. "If the servants or anyone else can't continue on after we get to Speck, we'll just leave them there and bring them back with us when we return. They can even make their own way back to Bogwood on their own once they recover from their ailments, that is, if they should prove a burden. And I'm hoping nobody proves a burden."

Chapter Four

Katja stared down on the glorious spectacle of Empire City. The third floor of the opulent King's Dream Inn furnished guests with a magnificent view. The city shimmered like a million gemstones from the light of countless torches wavering in the evening darkness. Old wealth, new wealth, wealth yet to be realized, the riches of a lifetime waited in this one place for the individual smart enough to reach out and seize the opportunity. The good life and all that came with it. Anything was possible.

Footsteps approached from behind, breaking her reverie.

"Admiring the sights?" came a man's voice.

"Yes, the sights." Katja turned.

"Men don't have time for such things." The man stepped out onto the balcony. His eyes shone with excitement as his gaze swept her form.

"You mean you were too busy swilling grog in a pub." She waved her hand in front of her face. "You reek like a keg, Crokus."

The big Scythian warrior, owner of Mercenary Company Sixteen, frowned. "You shouldn't speak to me in such tones. In my homeland—"

"Don't give me that," Katja said. "In Scythia, a woman would give you a good beating with a rolling pin for spending the day gambling and drinking, instead of tending to my needs." She managed a tone of righteous indignation despite making the story up on the spot. "Don't play me for a fool."

Crokus shook his head as if to clear it. "I . . . what?"

"Enough of your excuses. We need to talk business."

"What about?"

"I made contact with a patron today, a potential patron at any rate. The company stands to make a sizable remuneration."

Crokus blinked but said nothing.

"We stand to make a lot of money," Katja said. "A small fortune." She held out the gold coin provided by the foul-smelling magician.

"Who's the patron?"

"Does it really matter?"

Crokus's eyes narrowed. "Yes, always it matters, especially in times of uncertainty and war and such. No fee is worth getting my throat cut over, or being crucified."

"But the Empire isn't at war, that's my point. The work we do these days is all security stuff, catching criminals and the occasional troll and the like. No risk of crucifixion there."

"Who's the patron, Katja?"

"The truth is, I don't know who it is, not his real name. A person who choses to remain anonymous but has a lot more of these."

She placed the coin in Crokus's hand, half expecting the man to begin salivating like a dog.

"How much more?"

"One-hundred gold pieces. A nice slice of King Dexter's horde. Look at the stamp, it's legitimate."

Crokus held the coin close to his face. A line of spittle ran down his chin.

"What do we have to do for this patron?"

"We guard a horse up to the day of the big race." She smiled. "Ensure that no harm comes to our patron's steed at the Summer Festival."

"That's all? Why does he care so much about this beast's fate? Is he a gambler?"

She nodded. "He has wagered very heavily on the race, very heavily, so much so that he cannot afford to lose. The gold he's paying us is insignificant by comparison."

"Which team?"

"The red team. We guard the animal until the race begins, and then the gold is all ours."

"Why a mercenary troupe? This patron could hire regular guards for a fraction of the price."

She shrugged. "Perhaps he feels that common guards can be bought off easier, or that they're less apt to pay attention to their duties. Anyhow, I have the contract for the service right here." She snatched a rolled parchment from her waistband and held it out. "It just needs your signature."

Crokus frowned. "You made this entire deal without consulting me first? You overstep yourself, woman."

"Don't be a fool. There is no deal until you sign the contract. There hasn't been enough work lately for the company, and you know it. You were busy getting drunk and gambling with your friends and weren't around to ask, and I didn't want to turn down the funds. For shame."

Crokus slumped against the balcony railing. "True, we need the work. A hundred gold pieces you say? That would help get us through until next year."

Katja whispered next to his ear. "You're just lucky that I'm around to take such good care of you."

Chapter Five

"The servants are nothing but a burden. They're staying in Speck."

Gerald fought to keep his frustration from showing as the royal column struggled mightily on only the third day after leaving Bogwood. Even as he watched, a cook collapsed and lay unmoving on the road, the fifth casualty of the day. So far.

The Cypress trees, so plentiful in North Bogsonia, dwindled in size and number as they followed the road ever farther southward. Barren ground increasingly replaced the lushness of the swamp. A light breeze blew in from the direction of the Blasted Lands, dousing the party with bone-dry air.

Rogan hollered an order. A pair of guards rolled the fallen man atop a canvas sheet and proceeded to drag him down the road. Gerald frowned: the drummers, flag bearers, and even a few soldiers wavered unsteadily on their feet. The road ahead twisted in the direction of the Blasted Lands, promising the worst was yet to come. A porter stumbled and fell, and Gerald decided that he had seen enough.

"That's good for today, Rogan. Let's make camp."

The land came to life as the sun set. Clouds of insects large and small massed around the cook fires. Bats flittered through the air, smallish, regular sized bats, Gerald noted with approval. Audible above the crackling of the burning wood, insects clacked, chirped, and otherwise created a steady racket. Even a few toads sang in the darkness, though how anything could eke out a living in such an inhospitable place seemed a mystery.

"I should perhaps record the impressions of our leader for the sake of posterity," Parrot suggested.

"It was a poor day." Gerald shoved the last morsels of his meal into his mouth. "The health difficulties among the troupe have complicated our journey. You can quote me on that."

"Right." Parrot scrawled on a parchment. "A poor day."

"Right." Gerald reconsidered. "Well, no need to be negative. The king will be reading the report after all. Let me think of something else, something more natural."

Parrot watched impassively.

"We shall endeavor to persevere," Gerald said. "Yeah, that's better. Despite the trials and tribulations that have crossed our path, we shall endeavor to persevere. You can use that."

"Uh, thanks." Parrot frowned and scrawled on the parchment.

Gerald smiled. "We haven't seen any trolls for much of the day, which is nice."

"They all moved to the area around Bogwood." Rogan joined them at the fire. "Or maybe it just seems that way."

"Can't say as I blame them if this place is the alternative," Gerald said.

"I'm surprised to see you still on your feet, chronicler," Rogan said.

"I'm sitting, not standing."

"Still conscious, then."

"We scribes are a tough lot." Parrot smiled. "Even if we don't look it sometimes."

"You don't ever look it," Rogan said.

Parrot waved his hand through the air in a parody of writing. "Rogan and his men were drunk and in ill temper once again."

"Don't you dare write that," Rogan said. "I haven't been drinking nothing except water. You can't write it if it isn't true."

Parrot shrugged. "Maybe it's my version of the truth."

"You liar," Rogan said.

"Enough." Gerald waved a finger in the air. "The next man that argues on this trip gets thrown into the fire."

The banter died away at once.

Parrot coughed. "Perhaps this is a good time to continue our interview?"

"What else do you want to know?" Gerald said.

"How do you feel about attending the Emperor's birthday celebrations?"

Gerald could not help but laugh. How to comment on a birthday party thrown for a grown man? Yet the sight of the chronicler's hand hovering over the parchment left him choosing his words carefully.

"A great honor. There's really huge excitement for me in all this. I can't even describe it."

"Regarding your earlier comments on this being a poor day," Parrot said. "Are you looking for an improvement in the days to come?"

"You know," Gerald said, "I'm beginning to think it'd be a good idea if I were to regulate all this constant chronicling. Maybe I should designate certain times and areas off-limits."

"You could send him back to Bogwood," Rogan said. "Make the entire trip off-limits."

"King Gerald instructed me to come." Parrot turned back to Gerald. "When do you anticipate reaching Speck?"

"Two days," Gerald replied. "Despite being forced to carry those who can no longer walk, we should be in Speck around two days from now. That is, just so long as the rest of the column holds up."

Nobody replied.

Chapter Six

The red dragon stared.

A party of human travelers walked in a long line along the river valley below, moving slowly, heads down, completely exposed to attack from above. Like sheep lined up for the slaughter. Litters bore the fallen members of their crew. The dragon slavered in anticipation of an easy meal.

Claws clicked over bare rock as he shuffled clear of the stone overhang in front of his cliffside home. He opened and snapped shut his jaws several times in quick succession, working the bulging muscles along his maw in preparation for battle. He cinched tight the leather straps on his jacket of plate armor and tipped back the metal helm atop his head.

With a single flap of his wings, he sailed into the sky.

For but a bare moment did the dragon allow himself a small indulgence, a heartbeat of time in which to relish the sheer pleasure of flying, that indescribable sensation of riding the air under one's own wings, the updrafts, the scents, the warming sun on his back. A rumble in his belly brought his thoughts back to the present, and he stared hard at the men, using dragonsense to see more than mere eyes alone could discern. Not a one of them carried a crossbow, though at least two had bows across their backs and several others were armed with swords. The dragon nearly smiled as he drew back his wings and dropped through the air like a stone.

Wind whistled against his ears. The ground rushed nearer by the moment. He closed in on the men like a bolt of lightning. A likely target presented itself, a lone human staggering off to the side of the main group, a pack riding high atop its back. The dragon extended his claws and braced for impact.

The man tripped and fell flat on the ground.

The dragon tried desperately to correct his course, extending his wings and twisting his torso in a panicked attempt to pull out of the dive. Too late, a thorn bush smote him a mighty blow across his chest, and before he could recover, a stout branch rattled off his helm. Instinct prodded his wings to fold protectively against his back, and he slammed hard against the ground, the force of the impact driving the breath from his body. For long moments he could only lie still, sucking in one great lungful of air after another. A human rushed up to his side. The man's sword glistened in the sun. The dragon tried to stand but could do no more than twitch his legs. An ignominious end.

"It's not a bat after all," the human said. "It's some kind of a . . . mutant chicken. It must have flown out of control. Probably can barely get off the ground, just look at it."

The red dragon could scarcely believe his ears: a chicken?

"Fire and brimstone, are you mad?"

The man jumped back a full two paces. "By the bowels of the bog, the chicken talks."

The ground spun beneath the feet of the red dragon as he forced himself upright. The kiln in his chest burned hot, but his knees felt fretfully weak. He flexed the muscles along his breastbone, compressing the air in his lungs. He took aim at a nearby bush and exhaled in a forceful blast. To his surprise, only a stream of hot air escaped.

"Now it's hissing at me," the human said.

"I'm not a chicken," the dragon said. "And I wasn't hissing at you. That was supposed to be a burst of flames. I must be dazed."

"You're about the size of a chicken," the human insisted. "Are you sure you're not one?"

A second human walked up to the first man. "It's talking?"

"It is, my prince. But it insists it's not a chicken."

"Chickens can't talk," the dragon said. "I have scales in case you haven't noticed, not feathers. And teeth, see?" He barred his teeth.

"A mutant chicken, then," the first human said.

"I am Thundar the Magnificent," the dragon said. "Master of the Sky, King of the Winds, Blower of Fire, and holder of many other equally impressive titles. I am a red dragon."

The first human laughed rudely. "A dragon? A little wee one? Who's going to be afraid of you aside from a rabbit? Why are you dressed up like a soldier with a little helmet and a cape and such? And how come you can talk?"

Thundar stretched his wings wide. "Not so little."

The man laughed yet again. "You're only as high as my knee. Prince Gerald, I think perhaps an accursed magician is playing a grand jest on you and your servants."

"Put your sword away," Gerald said. "No need to kill it." He walked up to Thundar. "How come you can talk?"

"All dragons can talk."

Gerald shook his head. "I was taught that all dragons died during the Crazy Wars."

"Not all." Thundar said. "Obviously."

"This creature is known as a minor dragon," said a man in a white tunic. "For obvious reasons, they are also known as dwarf dragons. The major dragon lines were all wiped out long ago. Your schoolmasters were correct in that much at least."

Gerald nodded. "Why did you crash? Are you sick?"

"I . . . well . . . ." Thundar searched his mind for an acceptable answer. "Not sick, no. Downdraft back there. Lost all lift in my wings. Lucky I even managed to swerve and avoid crashing into somebody."

Still another human joined the others. He held a naked axe in his hands and a dangerous gleam in his eyes. A warrior.

"It looked to me like that thing was in a dive," the man said.

"A dive, Rogan?"

"Kind of, yeah. Like it was making a grab for that porter's pack but missed."

Thundar snorted indignantly. Twin jets of flame shot from his nose.

"Sure. Now it works."

"What?" said the warrior.

"Nothing."

"Is what Rogan says the truth, Thundar?" Gerald said. "You were about to attack my man? To steal his supplies?"

"Steal his sup . . . ?" Thundar scoffed. "Do I look like a vulture? Or an eagle? Dragons hardly need to pilfer the supplies of lesser beings to fill their bellies, of that you can be sure."

"Your ribs are showing along your flanks," Gerald said. "You look thin. Your tunic is drooping."

"I've been dieting," Thundar said. "Obesity is a problem among my species. And this land is suffering from a drought. There's not much food to be had, no matter how proficient the hunter. And what do you know about whether a dragon if fat or thin? You just said yourself that you've never seen one of my kind before."

"You've got me there."

"I crashed, that's all. Sorry for the inconvenience, but I should probably be getting along now. My mate is waiting for me back at the cave."

Much to Thundar's surprise, Gerald only nodded.

"Away with you then. Better luck with your flying in the future. Try not to hurt yourself."

Gerald and the others set off down the road. Porters and servants picked up their respective loads and followed.

Thundar called to the nearest human. "To where are you bound?"

"Empire city," replied the man. "To honor the Emperor."

"So far?" Thundar attempted a low whistle, but flames erupted from his mouth instead. He coughed. "So far? A long journey for a party so large as this. Some of your crew appear stricken with sickness."

"Don't even get me started on that," came the man's odd reply. "You talk to Rogan or Prince Gerald if you got something to say."

Thundar folded his wings against his back and raced down the road, weaving between the long human legs in his path. A booted foot nearly stomped on his head, and only a quick sidestep saved him from serious embarrassment.

"It does look like a chicken when it runs," Rogan said.

Prince Gerald nodded. "Is there something you want, Thundar? I thought you were in a rush to get back home?"

Thundar stamped his feet. "I am, but I was wondering if your company might need a scout for the remainder of your journey? I was about to set out on such a travel myself, and it just so happens that you're going my way. In return for food, I could provide you with aerial reconnaissance as you make your way to Empire City. Much safer for you and your people that way."

Gerald's eyes went wide. "You know, that just might help. What say you, Rogan?"

The warrior's dark expression grew even more dour. "I don't think we need him. I didn't get the impression that he could fly too good back there, and I don't see as how it'll help us with his crashing all over the place. Might scare off some enemy if it crashed directly into them I suppose, but that seems like a long shot."

"The crash was highly unusual," Thundar said. "Really rare event, purely the result of a freak set of circumstance that almost certainly will never arise again."

"Aerial reconnaissance could help us greatly," Gerald said. "Greatly."

"Yes," Rogan said. "You're right, of course. I suppose it's foolish to deny the obvious. It's just that I don't want to see our party in jeopardy because we decided to rely on the scouting reports of a chicken."

"What about your mate, Thundar?" Gerald said.

"Who?" Thundar searched his memory. "Oh, her. Truth be told, she flew away last springtime, and I haven't seen her since. We weren't getting along too well anymore, not for these last few years, so it was probably for the best."

"Females are a hard lot to please," Rogan intoned. "Maybe you should come along with us after all. Poor fellow. You've probably been through a lot."

"We'll reach the town of Speck in a couple of days," Gerald said. "If our agreement doesn't work out by then, we can go our separate ways. You have all of two days to prove yourself, dragon."

"A wise decision," Thundar said. "So, when is eating time?"

Chapter Seven

Zirac stared down on the wretched hovel known as Empire City. It depressed him to see so many useless people living such pathetic lives. They needed to be controlled, to be molded into useful vassals. Though it sullied his hands to associate with such human chaff, if only to use their worthless hides to further his own ends, even the greatest sorcerers of the ages had done the same when necessity dictated, and he was every bit as good and resourceful as they had been. Probably better.

"The woman has arrived," came the waif's message.

"Send her in." Zirac frowned. Speaking of pathetic . . .

"There you are." Katja tromped into the room. "Where's my gold? Crokus won't agree to the job if he finds out the company is working for you, but the sight of the gold just might get his mind off the identity of our patron and back on profits."

"The day of the race, Katja, then you will receive your chest of coins," Zirac said. "Provided my requests are carried out. Whether or not you choose to skip town with the treasure is entirely up to you."

Katja nodded. "Crokus also doesn't know you're planning to fix the big race. That alone could get us executed if the authorities were to find out. I'm beginning to have second thoughts myself."

"I trust you didn't tell him about the second part of our deal?"

"No, and he must not find out. He thinks we've been hired for guard duty, nothing else."

"It's nothing you can't pull off," Zirac soothed. "Nobody can or will ever try to connect you to anything. Just don't get caught."

"Easy for you to say."

Zirac withdrew a tiny glass vial from one of the dozens of pockets lining his robe.

"Make sure you do it right," he warned. "The powder must be mixed in with the horse's food or water. Not the vial, but the contents."

Katja deposited the vial in a front pocket of her tunic.

"Won't the yellow team just replace the affected horse with one that's not sick?"

"They certainly will if they detect that something is wrong, which is precisely why we're using this special powder. Trust me, the stuff has a visible effect on a horse only when it tries to run. It makes the beast all groggy and slow for a while, but remains in the body scarcely longer than the duration of a race. Nobody will ever know."

"What is it? Where did you get it?"

"Some friends brought it to me from afar. Remember, the contents of the vial must be consumed. Sprinkling it on the horse's hide won't do a thing."

"I got it," Katja said. "You're confident Councilor Lewis has wagered big on this race?"

Zirac smiled sagely. "I am. His gambling debts are said to be enormous. As things stand, he is barely keeping his head above the financial torrents seeking to suck him down. Following one more big loss, he will be ruined, truly destitute, and left with no option but to resign his position on the Council of Advisors."

"You have a man waiting to take his place?"

"Of course. Why else would I be doing this?"

Katja nodded. "And this new advisor will steer the Emperor toward a more lenient policy with magicians? Starting with rescinding your own expulsion?"

"That'll be first on the list, yes. Do your job properly and if all goes well, perhaps my man will also throw in a kind word to the Emperor regarding the mercenary companies."

"That would be swell. I always knew I could trust you, Zirac. When it comes right down to it, you and I aren't all that different after all."

Zirac stamped up the stairway.

That ill-dressed, perfume-drenched, cheap harlot of a woman! Comparing herself to him. They weren't that much different, she said. He could hardly believe her idiocy.

Did he go prancing around in a tunic that showed off more of his body than it rightly covered up? Did his bosoms go bouncing all over the place so that a man grew so distracted that he could hardly think straight or even sleep at night? It all made him so angry that he . . . he sought to relax. To push the disturbing thoughts from his mind. To refocus.

The waif hovered near as Zirac entered his lair. He shooed the creature away with a wave of his hand. Scrolls and parchments and leather-bound texts covered the top of his desk. He sat on his chair and cast a spell. A glass ball affixed to a pedestal in the corner of the room erupted in a glow of blue light. He winced and waved his hand and the intensity of the light softened appreciably.

A large jar on a shelf caught his attention as the creature imprisoned within moved. He picked up the jar to get a better look. A tiny, clawed appendage attached to a hairy mound of flesh and exposed organs scratched futilely at the smooth glass surface. A network of exposed nerve endings lined the creature's body. Zirac stared in pure pleasure. What had once been a powerful sorcerer, a rival to his own aspirations to become the head of the Wizard's Guild, could now only poke at the inside of a jar. It was a fate that made even the existence of the waif seem not too bad by comparison.

"The man you wished to see approaches," said the waif.

He placed the jar atop the shelf, sat back in his chair, and waited. Instead of the sassy demeanor of an uppity harlot who didn't know her place, the new visitor showcased all the fear and trepidation Zirac liked to see in his guests. The man's face shone with sweat, his eyes wide open, skin as white as snow. Sweat stains darkened the area of his robes below the armpits. His lips trembled. Zirac briefly wondered if the fat fool would pass out.

"Welcome to my home, Senator Page. Thanks for coming."

"Chamber of horrors," Page stammered. "Why meet you here?" He pointed back over his shoulder. "What is that flying eyeball thing? Monstrosity is what that is. Is it even legal to have in your possession?"

"Calm down," Zirac said. "The waif is from a different . . . dimension, shall we say? It can only exist here in these rooms due to some spells, but woe to the intruder that disturbs it. Its touch will freeze the life from anything in this world. Its orders are to protect my person above all else, so make no sudden moves toward me."

The clawed thing in the jar tapped on the glass. Senator Page's gaze shifted to the shelf and his face went slack. His mouth worked in silence.

"Never mind that either," Zirac assured. "It's just an old friend. I asked you to meet me here because we need to talk privately. My office at the castle is most assuredly safe, but the rest of the castle is overrun with visitors at the moment. You might be spotted leaving my presence."

"It's all because of the Emperor's birthday celebrations," Page said. "There's some function or other going on for the next couple of weeks."

"I hardly need to remind you that we cannot be seen together. What is about to happen must be kept secret, or all is lost."

"You won't double cross me, Zirac?" Senator Page stammered. "No offense intended."

Zirac blinked; the fat idiot made him sick.

"No offense taken, my friend, there will be no double cross or any other type of cross. Trust me. Who other than your loyal self could I possibly wish to see seated on the Council? After Senator Lewis is hauled away to debtor's prison in disgrace, I will work my magic and see to it that you are chosen to take his place. Persuading the Emperor to reverse his planned expulsion of sorcerers from Royal Court will be your first order of business, and convincing him that the Empire's best course lies in increasing the number of mages allowed to leave Wizardhome."

Page nodded. "Still, I'm just one person. The other councilors will also have a voice."

"Of course," Zirac said. "All I ask is that you explain to the Emperor the wisdom of your position."

"I can do that," Senator Page said. "But I'm not expected to be your puppet, right?"

Zirac glared.

"I mean, not on everything," Page added. "Of course I'll support whatever you say on all the magic stuff, but the rest, specifically the running of the kingdom and making decisions about which construction company gets the richest contracts. I'm my own man on that stuff. Right?"

Zirac nearly laughed aloud at the pathetic show of bravado.

"Of course you're your own man, Senator. Nobody around here has ever implied anything to the contrary. I just wanted to make my position clear regarding the magic issue, to be blunt, to be open with you about the favor I expect in return for setting you on the council. The rest I don't particularly care about. Enrich yourself and your family and friends as you will."

Page smiled, nodding. "Good, then we understand each other. You want to know something? Maybe we're not that different after all, you and I. Not that different at all."

Zirac sighed. "Indeed. Here. I almost forgot." He produced a glass vial from his robes and handed it to the other man.

"What's this?" Senator Page said.

"That is the means by which you will win the favor of the Emperor and ensure your appointment."

"Go on."

Zirac smiled. "In that vial is a substance called moondust. It's very rare. It has the odd property of making an average mug of wine taste spectacular, or a good mug of wine taste like the best in the world. After the big race, when the excitement of watching Senator Lewis lose is at a climax, you would do well to mix a little moondust in a cup of wine and offer it to the Emperor."

"The gesture would make that much difference?"

"Absolutely. It's an act that would earn the Emperor's eternal gratitude. When I suggest to him that you should take the place of Lewis on the council, for by that point it will be apparent to everyone Lewis is done for, the Emperor will remember who you are, make no mistake about it."

Page scratched his head. "Smart. That's a good idea. Thanks."

"Yes, but remember, only offer the Emperor the wine after Senator Lewis makes a scene, not before. Better yet, bring it over to the throne when I signal for you to do so. Until then, the Emperor is bound to be too distracted by events to even notice you."

"So then I told him that he and I are the same kind of people." Katja laughed so hard that she nearly fell out of her chair.

The pub swirled with activity. Soldiers, thieves, mercenaries, bodyguards, and others drank and argued within the vast interior of the run-down pub. Serving girls bore mugs of grog and spirits upon large trays. Candles at each table lit up the room in a dull glow. Men sucked on wooden pipes, exhaling great streams of acrid smoke. Katja took a long draught from her mug.

"This patron of ours found your comparison insulting?" Crokus said.

"He sure did." Katja reached over the table and slid a mug in the Scythian's direction. "Drink up, you're falling way behind."

"Just a moment," Crokus said. "I want to get this straight: Mr. Smith doesn't approve of you personally, but he thinks highly enough of my company to use us as guards at the Festival?"

"Right. I think he's probably heard what a great mercenary company we are, even if he doesn't like our kind."

"What is all this talk about our company? It's my company and mine alone."

Katja stuck out her lower lip. "I was just trying to help, to drum up a little business. I can't believe you. This is the thanks I get?"

Crokus shook his head. "No, nothing like that." He smiled and sipped at his mug. "It's just that the situation is unusual, that's all. I've never worked for a patron before that I never even met. Seems odd."

"I already told you, his identity must remain quiet for the sake of setting an example for his children. That they not know his gambling habits. It's nothing unseemly. I can't believe how you don't appreciate me. How you don't even care about all that I do for you."

"I appreciate it," Crokus said. "I appreciate it a lot. I just had a few questions, that's all. So what did this Mr. Smith say when you mentioned that you two are pretty much alike?"

"His face went bright red." Katja laughed again, unable to restrain herself. "He was all sour and insulted but tried to act like he wasn't. The guy has no idea what a bad actor he is."

"But we can trust him as our patron? To pay us?"

"So far as we can trust any other wealthy, scumbag noble."

Crokus snorted. "Not too reassuring, but true nonetheless. Your description pretty much fits all of them, especially the wealthy and scheming part."

"Don't worry about the payment. I've got that covered. The day before the race, I'll demand that he give me the loot. I'll tell him that it'd be a real shame if something were to happen to his horse. I don't think he'll blink at my demand with so much riding on the race. Trust me."

Chapter Eight

A shallow bay provided the seaside town of Speck a small measure of protection against the stormy waters of Lake Unpleasant. Gerald led the column down the main road through town, passing by a smattering of personal dwellings, outhouses, sheds, and smoke houses. A dozen men stood on duty in front of a guardhouse facing the sea. A lone guard squatted high atop a lookout tower, presumably on watch against marauding pirates. A modest fishing fleet consisted of a dozen scows at anchor in the dark water just offshore. Featureless, gray rock emerged from the water's edge to surround the town and beyond.

"What's that stench?" Rogan asked.

"Salt water," Thundar answered. "This lake is briny, no good to drink. Been getting saltier since the rain stopped falling a few years back. Good thing I'm around to tell you these things."

Gerald scratched his head. "The salt in the water makes the air stink?"

"Sure," Thundar said. "Salt in the air, salt in the water, salt in the land. Not much can grow around here because of it. You should know about stinky air. Your entire country is one big swamp."

Gerald laughed. "There's nothing unpleasant about the lushness of North Bogsonia, I assure you of that."

A single-lane road along the waterfront led past a small inn. As they approached, the front door banged open and a man of middle years walked out. A greasy apron encompassed his rotund torso. A frown twisted his face.

"What you got there?" he said. "That man sick? He carrying the plague? You people had better just keep on walking."

"No, not sickness," Gerald said. "Too much sun. They suffer from the dry conditions and lack of shade. Not a one among us is plague sick. And we have gold."

The innkeeper smiled and rubbed his hands together. "Then welcome, welcome, a big surprise to see you folks. I'm Joe, the proprietor, and this is my inn. Been kind of quiet around here as of late. Nice to have some company for a change. Make yourselves at home. There's room enough for all, bless you. The inn's empty at the moment, but that's not the fault of the food or anything else here, no sir." His face grew taut. "But I'd appreciate it if you'd leave that chicken outside. They tend to defecate wherever they please."

"I'm not a chicken," Thundar said. "Are all humans so hard of vision? I don't have any feathers, see? I'm a dragon, and my kind most certainly doesn't just defecate any old place. We choose our targets very carefully."

"Alright, but one accident and you're sleeping in the pigeon coup."

Thundar licked his lips. "Pigeons? That might be not such a bad idea after all. Where did you say this coup was?"

"Don't even think of it." Gerald turned to the innkeeper. "Why is your inn empty? Is the economy hereabouts suffering?"

"The economy is in trouble for sure, if you can call it an economy," the innkeeper said. "Them darn ogres raiding up and down the coastline means that an honest sailor hasn't been safe for some years now. Most trading goes overland these days, which isn't much. The fishing fleet catches enough anchovies and herring to sustain the townsfolk, but so far as luxuries go, the little extras like cloth and iron and other basic necessities, those are hard to come by. Oh, and travelers, those are rare as well. Planning on staying for a few days?"

"More than a few, at least some of us are," Gerald said. "I hoped to leave a good number of my contingent here until I return from Empire City. How much the cost?"

"No cost because it can't be done. I can take your gold for a night or two, but your folks can't stay. Like I said, things be tight hereabouts. Not enough food for all of you, not for any length of time."

Gerald looked back over his shoulder: the column effectively filled the interior of the inn. The fallen lined the floor. The able-bodied occupied every last table. Repeated requests for food prodded the innkeeper to retreat back inside the kitchen.

"What to do?" Gerald said. "We can't take them all with us. At the pace we're moving, we won't arrive in Empire City until four or five seasons from now."

"Send them back home," Rogan said. "There's no other choice. We shouldn't have brought them in the first place." He eyed Parrot. "Not that I'm being critical of the king, far from it. The man's a genius."

Parrot's eyebrows lifted as he scrawled on a parchment.

"My father will be displeased if we arrive at the Emperor's court without a full honor guard," Gerald said. "Though he'd probably like it even less if we don't make it to Empire City at all. Those are our options, a small group or none."

"We'll not miss the extra bodies," Rogan said. "Especially the so-called porters that my men have been dragging around these last days. By my count, of the fifty-four members in our group, fully fifteen are unable to walk at all. Incredible."

"You're forgetting about me." Thundar flapped his wings and hopped up on the back of Gerald's chair.

"You can't walk?"

"Of course I can walk." The dragon spread his wings. "I can even fly. I meant that there's fifty-five in the group now. You were forgetting to include me."

"Right," Gerald said. "Fifteen men on palanquins will require thirty more to drag their sorry behinds all the way back home, otherwise they'll be on the road until next winter. That leaves nine of us. And Thundar."

The dragon flapped its wings but remained quiet.

"I'd prefer to take along a couple of cooks and their assistants," Gerald said. "But sure enough, we'd end up carrying them around within a day or two and still have to do all the cooking and food preparation ourselves, and there'd still be mountains to climb. It'd probably be better to have a couple extra soldiers carry the Emperor's gift between them. So it's down to Rogan and six of his best men, me, and Parrot. And Thundar."

"Nice." Rogan waved his arm. "We're lucky to have made it this far with the likes of these in our company. Our pace will increase rapidly now."

"Did you get my name right, chronicler?" Thundar asked. "The tail end of the word is drawn out long, like an announcer introducing a combatant in a prize fight."

"What do you care?" Rogan said. "You're not even from North Bogsonia. What's it matter to you how you're written up in our chronicles?"

"I wish to be portrayed accurately." Thundar sniffed.

"I really should get some background information from you," Parrot said. "Do all dragons have a lair?"

"Pretty much," Thundar said. "All of us major species of dragons do, though some minor species roost in trees or caves."

"Like a chicken?" Rogan said.

Thundar nodded. "But usually we sleep on a bed. At least I do."

"What's it like inside a dragon's lair?" Parrot asked. "Gold and silver and treasure and such? Legends abound, but I've never heard a firsthand account."

"Traditionally, yes, there's lots of gold," Thundar said. "In the old days, many dragons managed to amass very large treasures. Literally filled their homes with booty of all kinds. My own lair is a touch more sparse. Been slim pickings lately, it's nobody's fault . . . ."

"It'd be fair to say you have a limited stash of treasure?" Parrot said.

"I mostly have sheep bones and the like." Thundar raised his voice to be heard above Rogan's laughter. "It's hard for a dragon to make a living these days. The dragons of old preyed on wealthy caravans and rich towns and on the herds of fat cattle common at the time. But the easy days are all gone now. Today a dragon's lucky to keep his belly from shrinking to nothing. The marketplace is brutal."

"The dragons doing the eating and pillaging were also a tad larger than yourself," Rogan said. "I can't imagine the likes of you attacking a herd of cattle or an entire town. Maybe you could steal a freshly baked pie from a windowsill but what else?"

"I have fought with hawks and eagles and other fierce beasts," Thundar said. "I drove off an osprey just yesterday. How have you distinguished yourself on this trip, soldier?"

"What of it?" Rogan scowled. "We just started out this week. I haven't had a chance to show what I can do yet." He lifted a clenched fist overhead. "As this chronicler is my witness, and the words I am speaking are being recorded on parchment, I vow to distinguish myself with my axe the very first time an occasion arises. This I swear."

"Did you get all that?" Thundar said.

"Yes, yes." Parrot scribbled furiously.

The innkeeper returned, trailed by a middle-aged woman and a smiling teenage girl. The younger soldiers reacted by tucking in wayward tunics and shaking back disheveled hair. Chests puffed out. The girl and the older woman seemed oblivious to the posturing as they glided table to table with the smoothness of long practice, efficiently serving food and drink while exchanging pleasantries with their new patrons.

"We've decided to send most of our people back home," Gerald said.

The innkeeper nodded. "You need to send them back or take them with you."

"They're going home. They will need to take most of our supplies with them so that they don't starve before they return to North Bogsonia. Those of us that are going on now need to find new supplies. Dare I ask the availability of a side of beef or a dozen loaves of bread?"

"No beef so far as I know, maybe a few loaves of bread. Some fish to be had. Probably get it at about a silver piece per pound."

"Are you serious?"

"I told you, supplies are in short supply. There's only so much extra to be had, and that comes at a premium."

"I also need to hire a boat," Gerald said. "A vessel large enough make a passage to Bandit with nine men and a medium-sized dragon as passengers. How much will that cost?"

The innkeeper's eyes bulged. "Be you joking with me now? With them ogres pirating everything they can lay their hands on? Why, you'd probably be talking around a hundred gold pieces, that is, if you could find anybody to agree to do it at all. All the money in the world isn't going to do much good if you spend the rest of your days in a slave pen in Smash."

"We're willing to risk it," Thundar said.

The innkeeper smiled. "You are a very brave dragon."

"I'm confident because we have Rogan on our side," Thundar explained. "He's big and strong and just recently took a vow to distinguish himself in some impressive manner. I'm looking forward to seeing some actual action out of him."

"You just wait, dragon," Rogan said. "We'll see who distinguishes what."

"It'll take most of our remaining funds to get to Bandit," Gerald said. "We can only hope that nothing unexpected happens afterward, else we'll be hunting the forests for our food."

"Nothing will happen," Rogan predicted. "It'll all go smoothly from here on out."

The innkeeper departed for a short spell and returned to report success in locating the captain of a small ship willing to risk the dangerous if lucrative passage to Bandit.

The following morning, Gerald saw the stricken members of the royal column and their porters off for Bogwood before boarding the ship along with his remaining men, Thundar perched on his shoulder.

Under full sails and clear skies, the old chartered fishing vessel plowed rapidly through the water for the duration of the first day of the voyage, and made even greater progress on the second day.

The storm hit on the morning of the third day out from Bandit.

Chapter Nine

Katja grinned and leaned back against the wooden rails behind the stable.

In the end, Zirac had been as easy to handle as any other man she had known. Despite the sorcerer's fearsome reputation, he remained still but a male beneath his smelly robes, complete with all the secret desires, insecurities, and laziness that typified men in general, and also suffered from the additional flaw of losing his nerve under pressure. He could only nod meekly when she demanded payment in full, despite her not having pulled off her own magic quite yet.

With the treasure safely packed away in her quarters, only the task of feeding the powder to the yellow team's horse remained. But how to get close to the beast? A heavy guard regulated traffic in and around the stables. One could not simply walk up to the yellow team's horse and feed it a potion. Or could she?

She left the red team's steed in the care of a pair of Crokus's guards and ventured through the exit doors and stared back over the grounds. The barn overlooked a field on the northeasterly side of the oval track. Grandstands circled the racing area, supporting spectator benches stacked thirty rows high. Trees and hedges and bushes and manicured lawns provided color over most of the non-racing areas of the complex.

Much to her disappointment, there seemed no obvious means of entering the yellow team's section of the barn undetected. The exterior windows remained shuttered despite the warmness of the day, and the service doors and hatchways closed. She debated making her way back inside and trying a different tact altogether, when a servant exited the barn through a side door and sulkily trod up to a wagon parked on a path nearby. He hoisted a jug atop his shoulder and slowly made his way back inside the barn, leaving the door ajar the entire while.

Katja crept up to the side of the wagon. The servant made another trip, evidently in an even greater funk as he tossed a jug to the ground and used his foot to roll the vessel up to the door. Katja raced up to the doorway and crouched on the far side of the door. The servant came back outside once again, dragging his sandals loudly with every step. Katja stepped around the door and slipped inside the barn unseen.

The dim lighting in the corridor forced her to move cautiously lest she run into something unaware. Every step took her deeper into enemy territory. Her heart pounded against her chest.

She might have worn something different, she decided, anything other than her usual tunic. She was not an entirely unknown person and might be recognized on sight.

As if to demonstrate the precariousness of her situation, a group of guards in yellow jerkins came tromping around the corner up ahead, moving straight in her direction. The fear of discovery spurred her to action.

She ducked down a side passage and wrenched down on the handle of the first door she came upon. To her immense relief, the lever turned, and she slipped inside and shut the door quietly on her heels.

Blackness. From within the room she listened as the guard's footsteps grew closer and closer. Men's voices became audible. The fear of discovery grew in her mind, and she considered throwing open the door and fleeing, making a run for freedom rather than allowing herself to be trapped like a rat in box.

The voices tapered away and faded to nothing. Katja took a deep breath and let out a long sigh. Her hand found the door latch in the darkness. She opened the door a crack, intending to resume her journey, but reconsidered: what if the room held gold or some other treasure?

She removed the dagger and flint from her belt and rapped the iron handle against the stone so that a stream of sparks fell to the floor. The resulting glow dully illuminated a small storage room, the shelves piled high with ropes, harnesses, halters, and other riding equipment. Junk. A tattered tunic dangling from a nail caught her attention. She slipped the garment over her head, taking care to trap her long tresses out of sight as well as to cover the daggers on her hips. A strip of cloth tied around her head partly shielded her eyes. A straw broom completed the disguise.

The dusty corridor led past a hayloft reeking of fresh cut alfalfa and then through a larger room where bridles and saddles and stirrups and leather goods hung from pegs set into the walls. The pungent scent of tanning chemicals filled the air.

She redoubled her pace. Would they kill her if she were caught? Might she claim her actions to be but a practical joke, a jest from Crokus? His sporting jab at the defenses employed by his colleagues?

She rounded a corner and nearly ran into a pair of guards. Rather than flee as before, she set her face in a determined expression and rushed past the men, her eyebrows furrowed and mouth pinched in a frown, altogether too busy with important business to so much as exchange a single word with the likes of them.

The bluff worked. One of the guards moved as if to block her progress, doubtless intending to to demand her business, but at the last moment he stepped aside. A thrill rushed through Katja and it was all she could do to keep from smiling.

She passed through yet another doorway and continued down a short corridor. She found herself facing a single wooden stable, the lone occupant an immense, chestnut brown horse.

The famed racing steed stood taller than she would have believed possible for any horse, a truly magnificent animal. Muscles rippled up and down its tawny hide. The straight, long legs led to bulging haunches and a chest nearly as wide as her outstretched arms. That such a creature could never be bested in a fair foot race seemed obvious enough.

She reached between the stable slats and poured the entire contents of the vial into the water trough in front of the horse and withdrew her hand in one motion. She hopped back to her feet and turned around, only to find herself facing a glaring guard.

"Are you supposed to be doing that?" The guard sounded angry.

Katja kept her head down and worked the broom across the floor. The unfamiliar device felt awkward in her hands.

"I was told to sweep, so I sweep."

"Whoever told you to come in here and stir up dust is a fool," the guard shouted. "It's my skin if anything happens to that horse. Get out of here."

Katja scurried up the corridor, all the while struggling to maintain an expression of fear while her heart sang in pure joy: victory!

A horrible scream erupted from the stable, and then another scream, and yet another, one hysterical peel of agony after another. Katja turned around.

The horse thrashed about in a frenzy. Despite Zirac's promises, the effects of the potion proved horrific beyond description. She was unable to look away as the perfect equine face drooped and bled to become a reeking mush, the eyes liquified to twin streams of gore, and blood sprayed from the nostrils in geysers of crimson. The steed shrieked one last time and collapsed, the perfect legs kicking spasmodically. Finally it lay still.

The guard held the point of his sword against Katja's throat. Other guards surrounded her.

"That wasn't supposed to happen," she said.

Chapter Ten

Gerald decided that surely they would all die.

Torrents of rain fell from the sky. Waves reared high above the ship, seemingly poised to come crashing down and snuff out the life of everyone aboard at any moment. The cabin amidships where he and the other passengers huddled provided the only protection available against the raging storm. The crew frantically raised and lowered the sails, their faces reflecting sheer terror. The ship bucked and heaved, charging up massive swells and hurling even faster down the backsides of the waves.

Gerald felt a growing unease in his stomach.

"I'm going to puke," he announced.

Rogan and Parrot and the soldiers scampered aside. Gerald lunged out the rear door of the cabin. The wind struck him full in the face, and he only just had time to turn his head before his stomach heaved. Rain soaked through his tunic in an instant. He panted and wiped at his nose with the back of his hand as strength returned to his limbs. A wall of water as deep as his thighs rolled over the deck. He held tight to the exterior of the cabin to avoid being swept away.

A huge breaker lifted the ship high above the sea, and for a brief moment the bay at Bandit and the safety of land lay in plain sight but a few miles ahead, and then they were speeding back down the wave, surging through the angry waters.

An unseen object struck Gerald from behind, driving him to his knees. He cursed and struggled back to his feet. The sight of the offending article, a large wooden crate wrapped in cargo netting, sent a shock through his system.

"Rogan," he hollered. "Give me a hand out here. The Emperor's birthday present is floating away."

The wind whipped away the words from his lips as they left his mouth. Nobody emerged from the cabin. The ship heaved precariously. The crate began to slide. He grabbed a hold of the cargo netting and dug in his heels.

A wave crashed over the deck, slamming him against the starboard bulwarks. He scrambled back to his feet. To his horror, the entire passenger cabin was gone, swept away by the power of the sea, disappeared without a trace along with everybody inside.

Another wave broke across the ship, and another. A cracking sound like the collapse of a tree preceded the fall of the mast. Sails and rigging fell into the sea and dragged through the water. The ship listed over and began to take on water.

A series of jagged rocks at the entrance to the bay rose above the sea like a row of serrated teeth. The wind drove the ship relentlessly toward the deadly monoliths. Gerald considered jumping overboard and swimming for shore, but a single glance at the savage water, a churning vortex of white froth, laid plain the suicidal futility of such an action. He wrapped his arms around the railing fastened to the bulwarks and held on tight.

The ship slammed against the rocks. A shock tore through the hull. Stout planks splintered like toothpicks. The deck split wide open. The hull buckled. Gerald held fast to the rail but found that he was falling anyhow. Then he was in the water, gasping, choking, and flailing his arms.

Gerald sat down upon the sandy beach and spat a curse.

"Has everybody else drowned?"

Rogan faced the sea. "Looks that way. We're lucky to be alive."

Rain fell in sheets and great gusts of wind blew, but the worst of the storm had already passed. Large waves crashed against the shore.

The wooden plank to which Gerald clung as he floated ashore flipped end over end in the rolling surf. Finding the plank represented a bit of luck that saved him from certain death by drowning. Others had not been so fortunate. Of the remainder of the crew and passengers, only a single pair of guards, Red and Skunk, numbered among the living, along with the court chronicler, who lay stretched out on his back in the sand, half drowned but still alive.

The Emperor's birthday gift was gone. The gold they needed to travel to Empire City was gone. Aside from the axe strapped to Rogan's back, most if not all of their weapons were gone. Their supplies were gone. Worst of all, many men had died. Gerald wanted to smash something.

"Harsh beginning to our journey," Rogan said.

"Harsh end is more like it," Gerald said. "Not much point in going on to Empire City if we don't have a gift for the Emperor. But how will we even get home again without coin to pay our fare? It's a long swim back to Speck."

Rogan shrugged. "Maybe we can work our way across on a ship heading back? I see no other means."

Gerald watched impassively as a dead bird washed up on the beach before he remembered that the ship had not included livestock among the cargo. He bent down and looked closer. The small body of Thundar the dragon tumbled in the waves, oblivious to the water now that it no longer breathed, now that it no longer lived. Gerald felt a stab of misery as he lifted the little body from the water. The dragon weighed next to nothing, mostly ribs and scales and skin.

"What have you got there?" Rogan said.

Gerald held up the corpse.

"By the sorcerer's behind, this has been a poor day." Rogan extended his hand. "Give me the little guy, I'll bury him. I'll not be leaving him for the gulls to pick at. He was alright. For a dragon."

Gerald handed the limp body to Rogan.

"I'll just dig a little hole and—"

Thundar vomited a stream of steaming water into the air, dousing the warrior's arms and chest. Rogan hollered and dropped the dragon on the sand and beat his hands about his upper body. Steam rose from his tunic.

"It puked on me," he shouted.

"I saw." Gerald knelt down beside the heaving reptile. "I thought you were dead."

"So did I." Thundar stretched out his long neck and vomited again. He groaned. "I might still die."

"That's great," Rogan said. "At least the dragon made it."

Gerald frowned. "You seemed unhappy about the prospect of burying our little mascot here just a few moments back."

"Mascot?" Thundar said.

Rogan nodded. "Forgive my foolish words. My heart is heavy for the loss of my men."

"And for the sailors." Gerald said.

"Right, them too. But what now?"

Gerald glanced up the beach. The town of Bandit stood only a couple of miles to the north. He estimated the time of day to be no later than early afternoon. Plenty of time to reach town.

"Have you any silver, Rogan?"

"None. Only my axe did I save."

Red and Skunk proved destitute.

"Dragons never use cash," Thundar informed. "Dragons take what they need."

"Parrot? Carrying any silver?"

The chronicler shook his head. "I was too busy breathing water to remember to bring any."

They walked along the beach in the direction of Bandit.

"We look like a pack of beggars," Rogan stated. "Rather than a royal column."

Beachcombers trotted past, heading in the direction of the flotsam washing up from the ship. Thundar solicited attention from some of the passersby, expressions that ranged from disapproval to open hostility.

"Have you ever been here before?" Gerald asked. "Or do these people simply not like dragons?"

Thundar shook his head. "I have never before entered this particular lair of mankind, but my people are the inevitable target of the bow and shaft in such backward places. Again, you forget the terrible damage dragons caused humans in times of old. Laid waste to entire towns, obliterated scores of soldiers . . . ."

"Again, those were a different type of dragon," Rogan said.

"You saw the looks on their faces," Thundar insisted. "They reek with fear. The memories of man are long indeed."

Rogan opened his mouth as if to speak but remained quiet.

Gerald placed Thundar atop his shoulder lest some stranger succumb to a primordial urge and stomp the dragon underfoot.

Bandit resembled a larger and more vibrant version of Speck. Situated at the foot of the Great Southern Pass and protected from the storms of Lake Unpleasant by a deepwater bay, the town seemingly held unlimited potential for growth owing to its location. Behind a stone seawall, a fishing fleet at anchor rose and fell in unison, the hulls clean and shiny. A series of brick warehouses along the high water mark indicated an economy more diversified than simply subsistence-level fishing. Single story and two story cottages provided homes for the majority of citizens, but here and there stood a huge estate, complete with proper glass windows and decorative security fences.

But all was not well in Bandit, that much was visible at a glance. Fearful and dour were the expressions of the few townsfolk walking about in public. Potholes lined the streets. The gutters were strewn with garbage. Signs of neglect grew more acute as they continued farther on. A collapsed barn blocked part of the road, and as yet there had been no attempt to remove the debris. Storefronts were boarded up.

"What goes on here?" Gerald wondered aloud. "What ails these people?"

"Here's a possibility." Parrot wandered up to a parchment attached to a stand in the middle of the street. "Reward offered for the person or persons brave enough to kill the Evil Dog of Dread. Reward: Five hundred gold pieces."

"What?" Gerald said. "Five hundred pieces of gold? That'd be all the coin we'd need for our trip to Empire City and then some. Are you sure it says gold pieces, not copper or some such?"

"I'm sure." Parrot crouched low in front of the sign. "Without a doubt. Right here, five hundred gold pieces."

"For doing what again?" asked Gerald.

Parrot cleared his throat and repeated his earlier announcement.

"All that gold for slaying a dog?" Rogan shook his head. "And this dog is a . . . dog?"

"I assume so," Parrot said. "Otherwise they'd probably call it something else, like a chicken."

"These people are afraid of a dog?" Rogan said. "That makes no sense."

Parrot rose to his feet. "Some dogs are pretty fierce."

"To an unarmed woman perhaps," Rogan said. "To a child. But to an armed fighting man? Ridiculous."

"The poster says it's an evil dog," Parrot said. "Evil. Probably a big dog with sharp teeth and all that. Viscous."

"But it's just a dog," Rogan insisted. "I don't care if it's as big as a pony, my axe will split its head in a hurry if these people are serious about this here reward. I can slay this evil dog and we can go on our way."

"Go, Rogan," said Red.

Skunk nodded vigorously.

"Finally, a chance to distinguish yourself," Thundar said. "Just like you've been wanting. And in front of our chronicler no less."

"You said it." Rogan smiled. "I care not the danger. I need only to know where this creature can be found."

A roadside cloth vendor supplied the relevant information.

"Looking to die are you?" the man said. "Fine with me. You be looking for a suburb on the west side of town. Just keep on in the direction you're headed. You'll find what you're looking for soon enough."

"Looking to die?" Rogan muttered as they made their way down the street. "These people fear so much?"

"Like Parrot said, it must be a fierce animal." Gerald pointed to yet another poster in the street. "Whoever put out these advertisements didn't want any potential takers to miss their opportunity. That's the third notice we've passed so far."

They moved westward. The streets and the houses became increasingly rundown. Nearly all the dwellings were deserted. Boards covered doorways. Pedestrians were nonexistent. Then only ruins remained. Collapsed roofs. Fallen walls.

Gerald began to wonder if they had lost their way and nearly suggested turning back, when he spotted a pair of sad looking guards approaching from the opposite direction. Chain mail drooped over their gaunt torsos. Scabbards dragged in the dirt.

Gerald smiled. "Ho, guards. We seek to win the reward for slaying the evil beast that beleaguers your fair town. Know you where this creature can be found?"

The guards' eyes widened simultaneously.

"Truly?" said the taller of the two.

Gerald nodded. "We mean to collect."

"Who?" the shorter guard asked. "Which among you is the chosen?"

"I will slay the beast," Rogan said. "With my axe."

The taller guard turned to the other.

"Jeb! Go get the Captain. Tell him an axeman intends to try for the reward."

The guard identified as Jeb ran off at a sprint and returned in short order trailed by a small contingent of horsemen in green tunics. Despite their uniforms, Gerald recognized the riders for mere townsfolk, the awkwardness with which they wore their swords and general nonmilitary bearing giving away their true nature. Part time soldiers, their main duties would be to enforce local bylaws and settle domestic disputes.

The shorter guard pointed. "That's the one, captain. The one with the axe."

The rider at the head of the column, a bowlegged individual endowed with a hooked nose and massive black beard, climbed down from his steed and approached Rogan.

"You truly intend to challenge the beast?"

"I do," Rogan said.

"Know that you must bring back its head to collect the reward."

"Of course," Rogan said. "How else? But what goes on here? None of your men have tried for the reward themselves?"

The horsemen exchanged uneasy glances or looked away.

"What good is gold if a man isn't alive to spend it?" the captain said. "There's no shame in refusing to throw one's life away."

"Over a dog?" Rogan said. "You look like a stout man. You be afraid of a dog?"

The captain frowned. "Who said anything about a dog?"

Rogan pointed. "He did. That guy right there. He said that a reward of gold is offered to the man who slays the evil dog of some such."

"If only that were so," the captain said. "Why, I'd go kill it myself. Somebody should teach that young fellow how to read. The gold is offered for the head of the one they call El Terrible, or Smorgen the Devourer."

Rogan frowned. "Not a dog?"

The captain laughed. "Nay, no canine, but the pet of a long-dead sorcerer, a demon from the abyss, evil incarnate, invincible and altogether horrible. The one they call the Evil God of Dread."

Chapter Eleven

"So that's why the printing looked kind of backward," Parrot said. "Sorry, Rogan, that'd be an evil god rather than an evil dog. My mistake."

Rogan's face took on a reddish hue. "Fighting a god is a lot different than a dog."

"No doubt." Parrot scratched his head. "Do I ever feel silly."

"What a great chance to distinguish yourself, Rogan," Thundar said. "Think of how this will look in the chronicles. It's what you've always wanted."

"Go, Rogan," Red said.

Skunk nodded his head.

"I was supposed to kill a dog." Rogan turned to Parrot. "You can't go and set me up and then put it in the chronicles as if you weren't involved."

"I write down everything that happens," Parrot said. "I keep a record of all that is said and done, including my own doings, with discretion of course, and using reason, as per the prince's orders. But what now? Are you backing out on collecting the reward?"

"Rogan wouldn't do that," Thundar protested. "He's not a coward, a yellow-bellied big talker but not a doer, like a mouthy eagle. He's been waiting on hot coals for the opportunity to showcase his bravery. How better to be remembered than as the slayer of an evil god?"

"But it's a god," Rogan said. "You heard the guard. A demon from the abyss."

"You are a brave man," Gerald said. "You'll be looking good in the chronicles now, regardless of the outcome."

Red and Skunk hollered encouragement.

Parrot scratched on a parchment. "Rogan agreed to slay the evil god." He stashed his writing quill in a pocket. "There, I'm done for the moment. Now to see how it all ends."

"This so-called god is causing problems?" Gerald asked.

The captain nodded. "It is holed up at the ruins of the castle of Sorcerer Dread, a mage as evil and loathsome as any that ever lived. His furniture was made from the bones of his victims. He had leather made from their hides. His powers were rivaled only by the might of his personal bodyguard, a horrible beast summoned directly from the pits of the netherworld. It still lives to this day, its powers undiminished."

"That's just great," Rogan said. "This just keeps getting better and better."

"And this demon still lives?" Gerald said. "Why didn't it go back to its own realm once the sorcerer died? Isn't that how these things normally work? This sorcerer is dead I presume?"

"Dread is dead," the captain said. "But the bodyguard has recently returned. Despite its absence for all the years since Dread was slain during the Crazy Wars, it is among us once again."

"Dread was a lucky man," Gerald commented. "To get that kind of obedience and loyalty from his people. Lucky him."

None of Gerald's subjects would meet his eyes.

"The beast comes forth to feed at night," the captain said. "As happened in times of old. The townsfolk have no defense against it. Why it is here again remains a mystery, but none can stop it. We appealed to Empire City for aid, but have yet to see any help."

"Rogan can do it," Thundar said. "No problem."

"The reward is to be paid in gold, is that correct?" Rogan said. "Not a dozen coppers? Our chronicler got that part right? Five hundred pieces of gold?"

"That's just being bitter," Parrot complained. "I mixed up a single word."

"Five hundred gold pieces is the reward for the head of the beast." The captain folded his arms against his chest. "Be you ready, warrior? Or be you having second thoughts on the matter?"

Rogan removed the axe from the scabbard on his back. His hands covered a good portion of the short-handled weapon. The curving, metal cutting edge gleamed in the sun.

"How many men have died before Rogan?" Thundar said. "I mean, how many men died before Rogan kills it?"

"I estimate slightly more than one hundred warriors have already died trying to slay the beast," the captain replied. "Those of my men that are still left haven't the nerve to even approach it. Not that I can really blame them. The first volunteers hardly provided encouragement for the rest, what with their dying so badly and all. All the screaming."

Rogan went still. "Screaming?"

The captain shrugged. "Shrieks, screaming, whatever you want to call it."

"Why not attack in force instead of individually?" Rogan said. "Strength in numbers is the first rule of warfare."

"We tried," the captain said. "Teams of warriors sought to slay the beast when this all began, but none returned."

"Those other guys probably didn't have an axe," Thundar said. "Rogan can do it."

"Easy for you to say, dragon. If you want to help, consider flying some reconnaissance and tell me what I'm up against."

Thundar shook back his wings. "Maybe I should be the one to fight this god as well. I do not fear. Did you hear that, chronicler?"

"You're not fooling anybody," Rogan said.

"Alright, then," Thundar said. "Where's this castle?"

The guard indicated a stand of tangled forest nearby. Among the largest trees, deep within the darkest shadows, a heap of moss-covered stones, black with age, loomed up like a low hill.

"Thundar wouldn't be able to see anything from the air," Gerald said. "Except for the treetops."

"The first rocks you encounter are only the beginning of the ruins," the captain said. "Merely the outskirts of the old castle. Your quarry awaits deeper within."

Rogan hunched his shoulders and swung his head from side to side. He repeated the ritual. And again. And once more. He bent down and touched his toes. Shoulder rolls. More stretches.

Red and Skunk began to fidget. The horsemen fingered their bridles and stared at one another. The captain of the guard opened his mouth as if about to speak.

Rogan nodded. "Let's get going. I haven't got all day."

Gerald suppressed a shiver as he stared over the ruins: the place stank of evil, ancient and malevolent.

"Good luck," Thundar called. "Dragonspeed."

Rogan walked a half dozen paces and came to a stop. "This beast can be killed by earthly weapons, can't it? Because that's all I've got, regular iron. If that won't do the job, then there's no point in my—"

"The beast can be killed by earthly weapons," the captain said. "No magic needed, or so goes the legend."

"Go, Rogan," Thundar shouted. "Don't forget to bring back its head."

The horsemen shouted encouragement. Red and Skunk hollered. Thundar blew a stream of fire skyward. Gerald cheered.

Chapter Twelve

"What kind of disturbance in the stables?" the Emperor demanded.

Zirac nearly clapped his hands in glee.

Revelers filled the Royal Hall to capacity. Highborn men and women dressed in expensive finery and laden with jewels and rare metals caroused with all the restraint of a pack of rabid sailors on shore leave. Dignity forgotten, if such a thing were ever a consideration in the first place, they gyrated their overweight bodies spasmodically to the discordant beats of the third-rate musical band.

The messenger leaned close to the throne. Zirac failed to hear the exchange above the general clamor of the party, but as the Emperor frowned and his face took on a reddish hue, the crowd fell into silence. The music stopped. The clinking of cups and plates and trays died away to nothing. Conversation came to a stop.

"There has been a problem," the Emperor announced. "The big race today has been sabotaged. A spy was caught poisoning the horse from the yellow team."

Gasps broke out around the room. Shouts of denial, cries of outrage, and demands for justice erupted from the crowd.

"I'm afraid it's true," the Emperor said. "The criminal who carried out this foul treachery is reportedly connected with a mercenary company. Hired to protect a steed, the fiend killed one instead. On race day yet. Most foul."

"Typical," Zirac called aloud. "Typical behavior from these mercenary troupes. They cannot be trusted. It is they who should be expelled from Empire City."

Seated nearby, Councilor Lewis shook his head.

"Sire, the mercenary companies are a generally trusted and reliable lot. If one among them has committed a crime, then that particular individual should be held accountable for his actions, but we should not let a single act by a single criminal color our thinking unduly. Maintaining order across the Empire is impossible without the law backed up by the force of the sword. Unless your highness is prepared to reinstitute the military draft, the use of professional soldiers is the only means by which to preserve order and security."

The Emperor shook his head. "I don't know, I don't know. It seems to me that these hired soldiers cause a lot of problems and solve relatively few. I'm wondering if Zirac isn't right this time, that banning the mercenary companies would be a good first step in taking the Empire in the direction of permanent peace."

"With all due respect, Sire," Lewis said, "Zirac is completely wrong. Imagine what would happen the next time the goblin and ogre armies crossed the Desolation Mountains and attacked the Empire."

"I don't know if that's still a concern," the Emperor said. "It appears we may have entered a new chapter in the history of mankind. The Empire is at peace. No longer do we need to fear imaginary threats. These days, more people are killed in knife fights in pubs than are slain and eaten by ogres."

"Only because there are no longer ogres around to eat them."

The Emperor waved his hand dismissively.

"Tut, tut, the more I think about this, the more I'm considering it. Combined with a ban on personal weapons, we could have some real peace around here for a change."

"That would be disastrous, Sire," Lewis said. "Leaving the Empire without standing armies in the form of mercenaries combined with disarming the populace is a recipe for suicide. The people would be as sheep for ogre spits, flesh to feed their young. Slaves for their pens."

"You might have a point there," the Emperor said. "Hard to put too much trust in that lot. I'll reserve final judgement on the matter for now, but at this point it seems—"

Councilor Lewis toppled out of his chair and collapsed on the floor. His screams echoed through Royal Hall, one long peel of agony after another. Spasms wracked his body. His head snapped back and forth in a frenzy. Black foam sprayed from his mouth. Where the councilor's eyes had been, only red gore remained.

Zirac stifled a giggle at the sight.

Pandemonium erupted in the hall. Partygoers fled in a hundred different directions. Men and women were trampled underfoot and crushed against door jambs by a crowd seeking to force its way through a handful of exits at the same time.

Zirac could not help himself and laughed aloud as Lewis vomited up huge gouts of blood, spraying the white marble flagstones with a river of the darkest offal. The new poison worked faster and produced more spectacular results than he would have believed possible.

Still the show went on. Lewis's legs and arms beat the ground in a frenzy, then slowed, and finally, much to Zirac's disappointment, went still. A sweet stench filled the air.

The Emperor remained seated on the throne, his imperial features slack. The royal guardsmen moved not an inch. Across the room, Senator Page stared in the direction of the Emperor as if seeking advice on what to do next. Zirac made a drinking motion with his hand. Page waved his arms and bounded up to the nearest wine bar. He filled a goblet with a purple liquid. The vial of moondust flashed whitely in his hand.

Zirac slid up to the side of the throne. "Forgive my intrusion, Majesty, but I must speak my mind and point out that this terrible act against Councilor Lewis was in fact an attempt on your own life."

The Emperor's eyes went wide. "What?"

"Your life, Sire, I fear that the attack on Councilor Lewis was meant for your royal self. That was no natural death. Lewis was poisoned, just look at the body."

"Poisoned. Yes." The Emperor stammered. "Obviously. Horrible."

Zirac lowered his voice to a whisper. "Your men should be protecting you at a time like this. Why are they just standing there?"

The Emperor seemed incapable of grasping the unexpected turn of events. His mouth worked but no words came forth.

"The poison was meant for you, I'm sure of it," Zirac said. "Remember the horse from the yellow team killed earlier today? There must be a larger conspiracy afoot. Did the servants mention the effects of the poison used on the horse?"

The Emperor shook his head. "No, only that . . . the horse's insides somehow melted. Yes, that it bled out of its eyes and mouth before it died, just like Lewis." He shuddered. "Who would want to do such a thing? To me of all people? I am their beloved monarch."

"Enemies," Zirac said. "Haters and control freaks. Liars. Who knows how far this thing goes? A man on the throne such as yourself, an honorable ruler concerned with the plight of the average citizen, your benevolent rule is an insufferable affront to them. They're willing to do anything to force their own narrow agenda on everybody else."

"But who? Specifically?"

"Bad guys." Zirac pointed. "Here comes one now. My intelligence tells me that he is one to watch."

"Who?" said the Emperor. "Which one?"

Zirac had to stifle a laugh as Senator Page came bounding up to the throne, his bovine eyes bright, cheeks rudy red. Rivulets of sweat ran down his face.

"My intelligence reported Page as a suspect, but I wasn't sure. Watch out."

Senator Page came to a stop in front of the throne.

"Sire, it is I, Senator Page. I wish to offer your royal self a special mug of wine. Chose it myself. Has a real special kick to it."

The Emperor recoiled. "Guards. Take him."

"Make him take a sip," Zirac whispered. "Then you'll know."

The Emperor's expression hardened. "Alright, Page. You take the first drink. On your life."

The senator looked bewildered but compiled with the demand, even smiling as he lifted the mug to his lips.

Zirac smiled inwardly. The so-called moondust was nothing more than the same poison used on the horse, and the same poison slipped into the drink of the recently deceased Councilor Lewis.

Senator Page screamed.

Chapter Thirteen

Rogan seethed in anger.

Parrot was a fool, he decided. How could a man get a thing like a dog and a god mixed up, especially when he was encouraging another man to fight the thing? A new idea sprang up in his thoughts, a possibility so startling that he nearly came to a stop in his tracks: had Parrot known the truth all along? That the reward was in fact offered for slaying a demon from hell rather than a lab or a spaniel or some such? He glanced back over his shoulder but was unable to pick out the chronicler's form among the others waving him off.

Enough whining, he admonished himself. You asked for a chance to shine in the official record, and there comes a time when a man needs to back up his mouth, even if the adversary turns out to be more than a renegade family pet. But a god?

He trudged between a jumble of massive stone blocks, giant slabs of granite weighing many tons each. The carved stones were worn smooth around the edges, testifying to great age. A waist-high brick retaining wall surrounded a black pit that on first sight resembled nothing more than an old water well. Then his gaze shifted over to a squat block of reddish sandstone nearby. Despite the passing of eons, dark stains discolored one entire end of the smooth surface in patterns like running water. A sacrificial altar, the device had been imbued with powerful magic to resist the scouring effects of countless seasons of rain and sun.

Beyond the last stand of cottonwood trees, the ruins of the castle stood in eerie silence. Not a single bird flew through the sky. No birdsong of any type could be heard. The ever-present whine of insect life was absent. Even the very wind seemed hushed, the scattered grass and thistle nodding as if manipulated by an invisible hand.

The castle had been almost completely destroyed at some point in the far off past. Building stones lay tossed about like child's play pieces thrown in a tantrum. Cracked and blackened foundation stones attested to the thoroughness of the devastation. Not a single outbuilding left standing. Devastation too complete and uniformly violent to stem solely from natural forces.

A wisp of smoke curled up from somewhere just ahead.

Rogan skirted around a pile of crushed rock, closing in on his adversary in a rush. Stealth abandoned, his chain mail rustled across his arms and chest and his booted feet clomped over the hard dirt. He skidded to a stop.

A stream of white smoke coiled out from a cave-like opening at the base of a hill of debris. Nothing could be seen within owing to darkness. Rather than succumb to his old instincts and throw caution aside and plunge headlong into the fray, he studied the scene a second time. Battle with a creature capable of killing one hundred men was one thing, but meeting up with it in utter darkness, quite another. That it possessed the intellect to use fire in a controlled manner left no doubt he was dealing with more than a mere animal.

The swirling breeze carried to his senses a whiff of a most horrible stench, a scent akin to rotting meat combined with sulfur and other foulnesses that he could not identify. The cave seemed certain to serve as the creature's lair.

He swung his axe back and forth, considering and rejecting options. Hollering a challenge seemed like the most direct approach, but he studied the cave entrance in greater detail again instead. Where was the door knocker? He switched to a one-handed grip on the axe and hurled a chunk of broken rock through the dark opening. No response. He made a second attempt to rouse the beast, flinging a stone the size of a small pumpkin into the cave, but again failed to rouse any hint of interest.

Fallen branches and dry grass lay scattered around the site. Never lowering the axe, he piled sticks in a big mound directly in front of the cave, taking extra care to stuff the spaces between the dry wood with dry grass and leaves. A single spark of flint set the mass ablaze. Flames took hold in moments. An armful of green grass atop the flames sent a stream of opaque white smoke pouring through the cave opening.

He moved to the side of the cave and waited for the beast to emerge, his axe held at the ready. Invincible was it? He smirked: a smash to the side of the head would test that theory rightly enough.

A stone rattled over the ground somewhere behind his back.

Rogan spun around, all the while cursing himself for a fool for having repeated the age-old folly of underestimating his foe. The god was not within the cave after all.

A huge swamp beetle closed in from ten paces away, having very nearly succeeded in sneaking up on Rogan without his even being aware of its presence. Digestive juices flowed from the obscene excuse for a mouth.

The situation struck Rogan as impossible even as he lifted his axe, that a creature of the deep swamps could be so far from its natural home, and residing in the ruins of an old castle at that, so completely outside of its natural habitat. And so much more dangerous than a dog.

The traditional Bogsonian method of slaying the swamp beetle flashed through his mind in an instant. Perfected through years of sometimes deadly trial and error, a successful hunter best provoked the beast to rear back on its hindmost legs and thereby expose its unarmored underside to the fury of a bow. But Rogan carried only his axe.

The beetle charged. The topmost arms along the grotesque thorax quivered like a double-row of tentacles. Mandibles the size of small tusks clacked together in a blur. Digestive juices poured from its maw. Despite a seeming awkwardness, tiny feet propelled the beetle at a rate about as fast as a grown man could run.

Rogan swung his axe in a blow aimed at the beast's head. A cracking sound like the snap of a stout tree branch preceded an entire mandible breaking clean away from the insect's face. Rogan brought down the axe a second time, and a third, and a forth, seeking to decapitate the giant monstrosity but repeatedly striking the edges of its body armor instead.

The beetle showed an inhuman ability to absorb punishment as it hopped to its feet and charged like a bull, and strruck Rogan a blow about the knees that sent him somersaulting through the air. He slammed to the ground, landing flat on his back. The axe slipped from his numb fingers. In an instant the beetle had him in its grasp, the hooked claws tearing into his tunic and scrabbling against the chain mail underneath. A broken stub of a mandible swung past his face, missing his throat by mere inches. He reached down to his belt intending to draw his dagger but found the blade trapped between his hip and the beetle. The ruined mandible ripped past his face a second time. As if understanding the futility of its actions, the beetle pulled Rogan closer to its face, trying to digest him externally. Mouth parts glistened wetly.

Fear lent Rogan a new power. In a feat of strength that in a less pressing moment might have given him pause to wonder at his own physical prowess, he tore free the dagger and slammed the blade up to the hilt into the beetle's face.

The insect wrenched back its head. The dagger snapped, leaving Rogan holding naught but the hilt. The beetle resumed its quest to pull Rogan up to its mouth. A drip of digestive fluid landed on his tunic, where it sizzled and smoked like acid.

Rogan pounded the hilt of the ruined dagger against the beetle's face, but to no effect. Abandoning the ruined weapon, he seized hold of the lone mandible in both hands and began twisting and turning, pushing back the misshapen head. The beetle shook its head like a dog shedding water, but Rogan managed to hold fast and maintain his advantage. He pushed and pulled. In moments his arms burned with fatigue, and still the beetle showed no signs of dying.

In a move born of desperation, Rogan jammed his thumb deep into the beetle's nearest eyeball, tearing a furrow through the rainbow-colored orb. The beetle swung back its head, clicking furiously.

He repeated the assault on the opposite eye, gouging out a large chunk of jelly-like matter, and if the damage was not quite as severe as his first attempt, the beetle reacted with equal displeasure, loosing a series of clicks and hisses and shaking so that it was all Rogan could do to maintain his grip. Claws that moments before worked to pull him inward scratched wildly in the opposite direction.

Rogan jumped clear of thrashing beetle and seized his axe. His other hand went to his tunic: the outer layer cloth was torn to shreds, but his chain mail had saved him from being disemboweled.

The beetle reared back on its hind legs, ready to resume the fight despite its injuries. Rogan attacked first. His heavy battle axe blurred through the air and struck the beetle about the knee, severing the limb. The beetle toppled over. Rogan's axe descended with power. The head of the swamp beetle rolled free from the thorax.

Rogan stood still for long moments, breathing deeply and resting until his heartbeat slowed. He retrieved the severed head, taking special care to keep his hands clear of the mouth area. An altogether wretched trophy, he decided, if but a momentary necessity to collect the reward of gold that came along with it.

"You killed my pet, manthing," a voice rasped.

Rogan turned around.

"You will beg for forgiveness, manthing, but you will squeal for a long time."

The goblin was large for its kind, nearly as tall as a man. A long, thin knife jutted from its hand.

"You will be sorry, manthing. You will pay with your screams. You will pay with your cries. Stupid manthing killed my pet."

Rogan lifted his axe. "Come over here. I'll be needing your head for the reward as well."

Chapter Fourteen

Zirac stared down on Empire City.

The search for the fiends responsible for the attempt on the Emperor's life continued without respite and on a massive scale. The entire army, national guard, reserves, and even the palace guard participated in the house to house search, leaving no stone unturned. Standing orders dictated that any sign of discontent or resistance among the populace was to be taken as an admission of guilt and dealt with in the most assertive manner possible.

Zirac laughed aloud.

"Get back off that balcony." The Emperor spoke from deep within the adjoining room. "Some fool might take a shot at you with a bow. Who knows how deep this thing goes? In any event, I can scarce afford to lose you now."

Zirac stepped back as he was bade. "Of course you are correct, Sire. Foolish of me to let my guard down. Men such as you and I, those of us who have nothing to hide, we tend to forget that there are others out there with a different set of priorities, a secret agenda. A conspiracy against the Empire strikes at the heart of everything right and pure in this world, and I find myself struggling with the concept."

"Don't ever think you're foolish," the Emperor said. "Suffice it to say that I've been dealing with these dishonest types longer than you have. Worry not. We shall find out all there is to know about this conspiracy in short order. Comrade Lentin has given me his word."

"Yes," Zirac said. "Comrade Lentin. I see."

The Emperor frowned. "What is it? Is there something you're not telling me?"

"No. Nothing . . . solid at that."

"Solid or not, if you have an opinion on any matter of importance, I'd like to hear it," the Emperor said. "Don't hold back now. You've already saved my life once, and did so even after I promised to repel magic users from my court. You I know I can trust."

Zirac lowered his head under the praise. "It is but the duty of every loyal citizen of the Empire to do his utmost to assist those wisest of men who govern it."

The Emperor nodded. "As it is every citizen's duty to counsel their Emperor when requested to do so. Out with it, speak your mind."

"Very well," Zirac said. "I am reluctant to bring this up, but I wonder if you can really trust Comrade Lentin? He's been the chief of the secret police for many decades now, but perhaps that's part of the problem? Why hasn't he arrested any of the conspirators yet? Why hasn't he uncovered the identity of the fiends behind the plot? Still no suspects other than Senator Page, a dead man?"

"It's only been a couple of days . . . ." The Emperor trailed off.

"My own intelligence tipped me off regarding a plot of some type," Zirac whispered. "Odd that a peaceful man like your court magician heard wind of this treachery before Comrade Lentin. Is he that out of touch?"

"I wouldn't go so far as to say that Lentin is out of touch."

"Then why hasn't he found anything? That's what has me concerned."

"I don't know." The Emperor scratched his head. "Who tipped you off? What was the source of your intelligence?"

Zirac waved his fingers through the air. "Admittedly, I had some help from the Arts, but even so, rumors were rampant among the serving staff that all would not be well on race day. I wonder if some of Lentin's own men aren't part of the problem, perhaps even the organizers of the conspiracy? It would help explain their utter lack of success in cracking the case. How many guards and servicemen involved in the search are secretly the plotters?"

"I hadn't thought of that." The Emperor spoke slowly. "I see your point. Lentin should have come up with something by now."

"With all the delays, whether intentional or not, I fear that those who plotted against your life may get away before they are caught."

The Emperor slammed his fist against the opposite palm. "They must not."

Zirac nodded. "At least you caught that wretched woman who poisoned the horse. The interrogators should spare no technique in wringing all possible information out of her. She is a central figure in this entire sordid episode, I see it clearly now."

"If only we could," the Emperor said. "That one escaped."

"What? Which one?"

"That woman who poisoned the horse." The Emperor shrugged. "She escaped from prison. They tell me she was under guard one moment and gone the next. We still have her partner locked up, a Scythian mercenary, but he knows nothing of importance, not even the identity of the patron that hired his troupe. It seems the woman arranged everything and played him for a fool. No point in questioning the man further. It's the woman we need to find."

Zirac choked down his anger. "Unfortunate that she escaped. It is my counsel she will create more havoc in the future. No effort should be spared to locate her."

The Emperor nodded. "Guards found a chest of coins in her quarters, tokens stolen from the Royal Treasury. We don't know how she got her hands on those either, but there's some speculation they were payment for the hit on the horse. In any event, the gold is back in the treasury where it belongs."

Zirac shook his head. "That scoundrel woman."

The Emperor nodded. "Do not despair. They will find her."

"I wonder how hard they're searching? Or how she got away in the first place? The entire situation seems exceedingly strange."

The Emperor frowned. "I'm beginning to think the same thing myself. It seems obvious that Comrade Lentin should have come up with at least a handful of the conspirators by now. Have I been living in a stupor?"

Zirac dropped his voice low. "I wouldn't be surprised if Lentin wishes to place himself on the throne."

The Emperor grew very still.

"What should I do, Zirac? I don't know who to trust."

Zirac lowered his head. "I believe it is safe to say that I have already proven my personal loyalty."

"Of course you have, and I've already said as much. Your counsel regarding the question of personal weapons has been especially keen, yet another issue that I so recently felt strongly about but in the opposite direction."

Zirac grinned. "It's for the benefit of the people, for their own good. What a horrible tragedy it is to have citizens injured and killed over nonsensical rivalries and petty squabbles. Future generations will remember your reign for its farsightedness and wisdom. For making the streets safe for our children."

A wisp of a smile crossed the Emperor's face. "I shall give the matter careful consideration. It helps to have loyal servants such as yourself."

"Then put me in charge of the secret service," Zirac said. "I shall find out all there is to know. I have ways."

"And replace Comrade Lentin?"

"For the good of the Empire. For the good of us all. Yes."

The Emperor pursed his lips. "A short time ago, I was ready to expel you from the court, but suddenly you've become like my own right arm. I shall consider what you say."

Chapter Fifteen

"It was nothing," Rogan said. "Merely a fairly heroic feat."

Parrot scratched on a parchment. "So was it nothing or a heroic feat? It can't be both."

"I was thinking the same thing myself," Thundar said.

"I only said that it was nothing," Rogan answered. "It's called humility. You should know without being told that my single-handedly slaying a swamp pincher and a goblin is no minor feat, even for a trained warrior."

"He's right this time," Gerald said. "Rogan did good."

Gerald's spirits soared with the column back on the road and once more making progress toward Empire City. The citizens of Bandit cheerfully paid the bounty on the beetle, funds that would more than cover the cost of a gift for the Emperor, new weapons, and any other expenses they might incur in their travels.

"We're really getting down in numbers," Parrot commented. "At this rate, I'll have nobody to write about before we get back to Bogwood."

"From fifty-four men to five and a dragon, just like that," Gerald said. "The people we sent back home were more hindrance than help, but the thought of those we lost at sea makes me sick to my guts. All for some birthday party."

They walked along in silence for a time, climbing one hill after another.

"Were there any riches in the goblin's lair, Rogan?" Thundar asked. "Future readers of the chronicles might be interested."

"Truly," Parrot said. "How say you, Rogan?"

"I did not enter the goblin's lair. It was dark as a grave in there. I might have stepped into a well or fallen down a bottomless hole. I'm confident the smoke from my fire would have driven out any more of them still inside." Rogan scratched his head. "What I'm curious about was this big stack of firewood piled atop a hill near the ruins. It was unquestionably intended for a signal fire. There's goblin footprints all around the place, and fairly fresh. You could just see the water in the harbor from the spot, and not much else. I can't understand why a goblin would go through the labor of building a signal fire. Who would it be signaling in the harbor?"

"It might have been shipwrecked," Parrot said. "Perhaps it intended to signal to a passing ship of goblins?"

"Are you new at this or something?" Rogan said. "Goblins don't care about other goblins. There's not a single goblin captain alive that would risk his ship to save one of their own. For that matter, any goblin ship that dared to sail into Bandit or any other human settlement would be attacked and burned out just as soon as it put ashore. Not even a shipload of trolls crazy on hooch would be that stupid."

"Ogres are renowned seafarers," Parrot said. "Might an ogre help a fellow evil creature?"

Rogan laughed. "Ogres got no use for goblins except in time of war, otherwise they burn them alive for sport."

Parrot shrugged. "But you found this signal fire all the same. If not goblins or ogres or trolls, who was the signal fire intended for? Seems like the only remaining candidates number among the human population."

Rogan frowned. "Unlikely. Extremely unlikely. What person would make a deal with a goblin? What could the creature offer a man in trade?"

"Something odd seems to have been going on," Gerald said. "That pincher certainly didn't walk here from the Bogsonian marshlands all by itself."

"That part is no mystery," Rogan said. "The goblin brought it here, probably when the bug was still a nymph. It called the thing its pet before it lost its head."

Gerald nodded. "Again, strange that a goblin would wind up the sole survivor of a shipwreck and still manage to save its pet bug, yet that's the most likely scenario I can come up with. Though even a goblin must have known that eating townsfolk would eventually get it caught and killed."

"Goblins are not a logical species," Thundar said. "It might have just acted on a whim and set up its lair where it thought the villagers would be easy for the taking. It wouldn't surprise me. They say goblin tastes terrible, sour and putrid even when fresh. Really disgusting."

"I'll . . . keep that in mind," Rogan said. "Most goblins are short and skinny, but this was a big one, and jiggling with fat. The swamp pincher was large as well, stout and strong. During my tussle with the thing, I tried to twist its head around and break its neck, but there was no way."

"A beetle doesn't have a spine to break," Gerald said. "You'd need to twist its head off to kill it like that."

Rogan frowned. "Says who?"

"Says anyone that's ever stepped on a beetle," Gerald said. "Look, it really doesn't matter. Did you mention the signal fire to the townsfolk?"

"I did. They seemed plenty interested," Rogan said. "They couldn't figure it out either, as to who the goblin intended to signal and all that."

Nobody replied.

The Great Southern Pass cut a narrow trail through the jagged wastes of the Desolation Mountains. Gerald led the way up the steep slopes, pausing often to catch his breath as the air became increasingly thin. At the summit of the pass, a deserted military fort stood a lonely vigil. Made from stone and sturdy by design, the structure would likely remain intact for centuries despite a lack of tenants.

"Why was the fort abandoned?" Gerald said. "It seems to be in good physical condition."

"The Emperor must have ordered it decommissioned," Parrot said. "The threat it was meant to counter must have been judged to be gone."

"Sheer idiocy if that's what happened," Rogan said. "The ogres aren't gone. They will invade the Empire again. It's only a matter of when."

"When was the last time an army came through here?" Gerald said.

"During the Crazy Wars," Parrot answered. "When the rock giants rebelled and closed off the Northern Pass, the ogres, trolls, and goblins came through this place. Following the war, the fort was erected as an early warning system. The idea was to put out the word that the enemy was coming before the ogres even made it through to the other side of the pass. Military units would fight a delaying action until reinforcements arrived from other parts of the Empire. Our vigilance has fallen away through the years."

Rogan spat. "Ogres and goblins have nothing else better to do than cause trouble, and trolls will go wherever a free meal leads them."

"I'll ask about it once we get to Empire City," Gerald said.

A thunderstorm rushed through the mountains the following morning. The increase in humidity that accompanied the rain felt soothing in Gerald's lungs and throat, left raw after days of breathing dry mountain air, but the rocky terrain grew slick underfoot and travel became treacherous. A stone overhang nestled among a bluff of rocks provided some tiny degree of shelter against the worst of the elements, though nothing could be done about the ear-splitting crashes of thunder, as arching beams of light crisscrossed the sky close overhead. Thundar complained that he might go deaf from all the noise, but the storm moved on sometime during the night, and in the morning they continued on without having incurred any casualties.

The road soon expanded and smoothed, improving in a few miles from little more than a path to a proper highway, complete with footprints and wheel tracks and other signs of traffic. A short distance farther on they came across a small hamlet, a mere dozen stout dwellings crowded along the bank of a wide stream but notable as the first town westward of the Desolation Mountains. Stacks of lumber and even larger stacks of raw timbers indicated logging as the main source of local employment. Parrot marked the event with a flurry of writing.

The townsfolk showed no outward signs of alarm as Gerald and the remnants of his column made their way through town.

"This place is at peace at least," the dragon said. "There are no evil dogs devouring these townsfolk."

"That was the dumbest thing ever," Rogan said. "Evil dog."

"Let it go," Parrot answered.

They purchased supplies at a general store. Along with axes and wedges and tools intended for use in the logging industry, the walls hung heavy with dried food and other essentials, including much needed flint for starting fires. The merchant behind the sales counter eyed Thundar suspiciously but accepted payment for his goods without comment or question.

A second village waited only a few miles down the road, and a short distance after that, yet another village, this settlement larger than the previous two combined. As the sun was about to set, they came upon a town so large as to rival the majesty of Bogwood. Gerald could hardly believe his eyes.

"It's incredible how many people live in the Empire," he said.

"This is just the beginning of it," Thundar said. "We've only seen little towns so far. Wait until you see the crowds in Empire City."

Chapter Sixteen

"Who are you?" Katja said.

"I am Pug, a servant in the Emperor's household. My apologies for leaving you here the other day without explanation, but this is my first chance to slip away from my duties since I rescued you."

Katja stared outside through a tiny crack in the stones of the ancient crypt. She shook her head: three days had passed since her escape and still the city remained in a state of uproar. Guards and army patrols repeatedly searched every house and warehouse within eyeshot of the cemetery, clearly involved in a manhunt. She could only presume the dragnet spread across the entire city. The locked interior of the crypt seemed about the only space in the entire area where the military had not yet conducted a search.

She glanced back at the boy who had saved her life. She was extremely fortunate, of that there could be no doubt. As she was about to be thrown into a dungeon, without the slightest doubt to be tortured and who knew what else, her young rescuer appeared seemingly out of nowhere. During a single moment when the guards were distracted by a game of dice, he had snatched her out from beneath their noses. A side tunnel as dark as a tomb except for the light cast by the boy's torch served as their means of escape. They came to a site of ancient catacombs. Only mouldering bones remained of bodies placed in recessed alcoves along the walls. Skulls grinned in lifeless caricatures of glee. Much to her relief, the tunnel ended at a staircase that ascended to the immeasurably less gruesome surroundings of the crypt.

"All this for a dead horse?" Katja marveled at the sheer number of guards involved in the search. Several dozen armed men marched up the street across from the graveyard even as she watched. "Who knew they cared so much?"

"Councilor Lewis has been murdered," Pug said. "Did you not know?"

"I did not. But what does that have to do with anything?"

Pug's expression turned somber. "They say that Councilor Lewis's insides melted away the same as that horse you poisoned. And when Senator Page offered the Emperor a mug of wine but was told to drink it himself instead, the same thing happened."

"What thing happened?"

"The Senator's face melted. His insides poured out of him. They all think you tried to murder the Emperor. Or that you were working for the person behind it."

"That stinking sorcerer is responsible for all this. I will denounce him."

"Zirac is now among the Emperor's favorites," Pug said.

Katja nearly choked. "I thought he was to be forced into exile at Wizardhome?"

"That is not going to happen from what I've heard," Pug said. "There's been a lot of changes these last couple of days, big shakeups. They say it's not over yet. Rumor has it that we'll be seeing a lot more magicians throughout the Empire now, rather than less. Every town is to have a magic overseer or mayor or something along those lines. Oh, and Zirac is now said to be the leading candidate for the position of the head of the Secret Service."

"You've got to be joking."

"Not at all. Comrade Lentin was relieved of his command and in shame committed suicide the same day, though some say he was murdered."

"So why have you helped me?" Katja said. "I appreciate being sprung from jail, as well as for the food and water you brought today. But what's in it for you? They will surely kill you if they find out you helped me. Why have you done this?"

"Well, I've seen you before."

"Have you now? I don't live in the castle."

Pug nodded. "You visited the castle on at least two separate occasions. I noticed you then. You seemed really nice, but when they said you killed the horse, I thought maybe you weren't nice after all. But then I heard a rumor that Zirac is fighting with Councilor Lewis on the council, and I remembered accidentally overhearing a couple of nobles plotting to do something and how one of them mentioned that Councilor Lewis's people would want an investigation after a certain thing happened. Then I knew it was Zirac that did it and not you."

Katja clenched her teeth. "I have been a very large fool. Crokus and his men are in prison I assume?"

"They were released," Pug said. "They were banned from Empire City on pain of death, but their lives were spared when it was deemed that you alone were behind the conspiracy to murder the Emperor."

"Murder the Emperor?" Katja said. "That's just insane. At least Crokus and his men weren't executed, though bad enough he was expelled. But regicide? I thought I was in trouble when they decided I had intentionally sabotaged the big race."

"Was it really Zirac's fault how the horse died?"

Katja stared at her young rescuer really well for the first time. The boy could be no more than fourteen seasons old, his shoulders and and arms painfully thin, still hovering on the verge of adolescence.

"Of course it was Zirac's fault. He gave me a powder and said it would only slow the horse, not kill it."

Relief swept Pug's face. "Since Senator Page is dead, you are the only one who knows where the powder came from."

Katja nodded. "Which means Zirac wants me caught very badly and dead even more. That stinking sorcerer."

"The weapons ban is to begin next month."

"What?"

"That was the other bit of news from yesterday. The Emperor announced a new law that makes it illegal to be in possession of any weapon of any type that can be used for offensive purposes, including swords, maces, spears, and all the rest. Only members of the army and officially approved guardsmen are exempt."

"Why is the Emperor doing this? Is Zirac behind this nonsense as well?"

"The servants say Zirac counsels the Emperor to pass the new laws. To smelt the swords into plow shears, I believe is his term. He conspires to create a lasting peace."

"Plow the land?" Katja said. "What a joke. Zirac has managed to wrangle a position in the Emperor's confidence using an emergency that he himself intentionally created. And I was his patsy, his stooge. If only I can get out of the city without being seen, then maybe I've still got a chance. I might go to Lowtarrif or Godtown, anywhere nobody's ever seen me before. My life here is ruined. That . . . magician."

"You are still alive. You might not be. Or you could be in chains and wish you were dead."

"Yes. You have done me a great service freeing me from my captors. My heartfelt thanks."

"A great service." Pug stared expectantly. "A great favor."

Katja stared. "My thanks."

"I know of a way you can repay me."

Katja nearly laughed aloud. Men had been falling over themselves in her presence since she was barely more than a girl. But would this mere boy have the audacity to request something untoward? Struggling to keep from grinning, she gave her best seductive smile.

"Alright, let's hear it. What do you want from me?"

"Take me with you. When you leave here. Take me along."

Katja crossed her arms. "I can't do that. I'm on the run, remember? I'm a fugitive."

"You even said they will kill me if they find out I helped you. Zirac will be especially angry with me. He would probably interrogate me personally. And the truth is that you remind me of my mom. She was a servant at the castle. She died a couple of years back from the chills. You look a bit like her and your voice sounds kind of the same."

"I remind you of your mom?"

"Except that you're older and . . . well . . . you have a bigger backside."

Katja was speechless.

"But that stuff doesn't matter," Pug said. "Take me with you. Wherever you go."

"I can't. I have to wait until things cool down before I go anywhere, and I don't even know where I'll go yet. I'll likely end up getting caught by the authorities regardless, but they won't take me alive again, not just to be interrogated by Zirac. Don't look so forlorn. Keep your head down and you'll be safer at the castle than to follow me. As things stand, nobody even suspects you, else you'd already have been arrested."

Pug nodded slowly. "I didn't really think you'd be able to take me, but it couldn't hurt to ask. I'm just glad I helped you when I had the chance. Mom."

Katja shook her head. "Don't ever call me that."

Chapter Seventeen

"This is the most deceptively named place on the planet," Rogan said.

Gerald forced his parched throat to swallow. The weight of Thundar atop his shoulder felt unusually burdensome. "My father's description wasn't that far off as it turns out, at least so far as this land goes."

The road cut due west, running straight as an arrow. Flat farm fields, green with waist-high crops, extended to the horizon in every direction. Small cottages set back from the road provided homes for the inhabitants of the state of Plenty. Not a single hill, rise, gully, or swamp interrupted the relentless monotony of the landscape.

Gerald spat. "It's as if the gods squashed everything around here with a giant spatula."

A plume of fine dust rose up from their every footstep, leaving a cloud of dust in their wake. An occasional shrub or willow grew beside a cottage, but not a single shade tree grew anywhere near the vicinity of the road.

"Plenty," Rogan said. "What a sick joke."

Red and Skunk voiced their agreement.

"The name of the land is Plenty," Parrot said. "It's a name, not a description, though in this particular case it serves as both. The rich soil and regular rainfalls combine to make Plenty among the most productive farmland in the Empire."

Gerald stared around, unimpressed. The cultivated crops, while so plentiful as to resemble an ocean of green stalks, left little room for anything else to grow.

"Regular rainfalls?" Rogan scoffed. "Says who?"

"The crops do, otherwise they wouldn't be so green," Parrot said.

"You guys are from a swamp," Thundar said. "You're accustomed to rain every day, but most places aren't that way."

"The plants are all of the same type." Gerald shook his head. "I would tire of eating the same stuff every day. Where's the variety?"

"They sell the crops," Parrot said. "And in so doing, feed half the Empire. Speaking of which, we are rapidly nearing our destination at long last. Have you decided on a gift for the Emperor on the occasion of his birthday?"

Gerald rubbed his chin. "I'll have to see what's available once we get to Empire City. At least we have the funds at our disposal to acquire something suitable."

"Just so long as the gift is practical," Rogan said. "I hate it when I get something I can't use, like a statuette or figurine or something equally useless."

Parrot shook his head. "That's just it, the ruler of the realm doesn't need a practical gift. What would our own beloved King Gerald V do with a shovel? You want to give the Emperor a present that represents North Bogsonia, something that helps create the image you would like North Bogsonia to be remembered by."

"Buy him an axe," Rogan said. "A good battle axe, you can't go wrong with a fine weapon. Symbolic and practical."

"Symbolic of what?" Parrot said.

"That you'd better not mess with the guy carrying it."

"I'd give the Emperor a whole barbecued sheep." Thundar licked his lips. "Best gift I can think of. Cooked rare. Yum."

"Ale," Red suggested. "A drum of ale. Or wine."

"Ale," Skunk agreed. "And wine."

"Practical suggestions aplenty," Parrot said. "But not very symbolic."

Gerald grinned. "I was leaning toward the ale."

"A barrel of booze is not an appropriate gift for the Emperor," Parrot insisted. "Just think how good that would look in the chronicles."

"Really good, I'd say," Rogan said. "On second thought, I'm throwing in with these other guys and recommending the ale."

Gerald nodded. "Just as soon as a free vote becomes law, I'll keep everybody's opinion in mind, or at least pretend to. But until then, I think I'd better choose something more symbolic. My father's intended gift certainly wasn't very practical. What use for a wood bust of King Gerald V?"

"That's what was in that crate?" Rogan said. "A wood carving of your father's head?"

Gerald nodded. "It was going to be a surprise."

"It sure would have been that," Rogan said. "Can you imagine being one of them porters? Carry that big package all the way from Bogwood to Empire City only to find out once you arrived that your precious cargo was a piece of garbage?"

"You don't like the gift?" Gerald said. "I thought to replace it with another of the same type."

"Rogan didn't like the Emperor's gift." Parrot scratched on a parchment.

"I only meant that artwork has no practical uses," Rogan said. "Fine idea otherwise. A bust of our beloved king, why, any man would be honored to receive such a thing, practicality or no. Anyone but a fool."

"A replacement bust will be easy to solicit," Parrot said. "Any reasonably accurate description of our king to a local artist should do the job."

The road switched from a dirt surface to a boulevard of interlocking cut stones, a boundary marking the outskirts of Empire City. Strangers passed by without so much as a glance. Shacks and tents and other structures dotted the landscape. Donkeys clomped past towing carts filled with a variety of goods. A foul scent in the air grew to a truly powerful stench as they passed by a makeshift tannery. Clouds of noxious chemicals shimmered over the workers stirring animal skins in vats of bubbling liquid.

"It's been no easy journey to get here," Rogan exclaimed. "I'm up for a bit of rest and a mug, if it be the pleasure of the prince."

"Of course," Gerald said. "Normally, I'd prefer to get our affairs in order first, to announce our arrival at the castle and all that, but after all that's happened, a mug of ale it is."

Parrot called attention to a message painted atop a door on the opposite side of the street.

"Paradise Pub and Inn, it says."

"Are you sure?" Rogan said.

"Let it go, Rogan," Thundar whispered.

The Paradise Pub and Inn had seen better days. The painted plaster facade was faded and cracked and crumbling away entirely in some areas. The place was deserted. Sunlight streamed through a row of open windows along the southernmost wall. A middle-aged man in a grease-stained apron stood behind a bar, staring and scowling.

"What's that on your shoulder?" he called.

Gerald walked up to the bar. "A dragon."

"Is it dangerous?"

Gerald shook his head. "Only to his enemies. Otherwise he brings good luck."

"I could use some of that myself," the bartender said. "Are you folks new to town?"

"We're here for the summer festival."

"You'll need to tread carefully."

"We're here to attend the Emperor's birthday celebrations," Gerald said. "Is there a problem?"

"You haven't heard? The summer festival is still going ahead, but some important men were recently murdered, and the authorities are still searching for the responsible parties. An attempt was even made on the life of the Emperor. Security across the city has been stepped up. Random searches are the new reality. The same goes for midnight raids and arrest without cause, all in the name of public safety. The Emperor is determined to stamp out any potential trouble, regardless of the form. He's committed."

"But the summer festival continues?"

"So far as it can proceed in an atmosphere of, let's face it, uncertainty and fear."

"Heck of a time to come for a birthday party," Rogan said. "Very festive."

"It wasn't my idea to come," Gerald said. "Besides, maybe we can aid the Emperor, and help him set things right. I will offer my services if I get the chance."

"A couple of blocks down the road from here you'll come to a police road block," the barkeep said, "one of many in and around the city. That's the new reality as well." His voice dropped low. "They say the Emperor has been corrupted by an evil sorcerer, a mage by the name of Zirac. This wizard has emerged as the closest advisor to the throne. He is described as evil incarnate, equal parts greed, ambition, and hate."

Rogan stared. "A heck of a time to come."

"You volunteered," Gerald said. "Unlike me."

"Send Rogan after this evil mage," Thundar said. "He's already killed an evil god. A mere magician would be barbecued pork chops by comparison."

"I think it's your turn, dragon," Rogan said. "Earn your keep and all that."

"I fly reconnaissance. We can switch jobs if you like: I'll stand around and talk real loud to my fellow soldiers while you fly ahead and make sure we're not about to be ambushed by a party of ogres or something similar."

"Not much chance of ogres in Empire City," Rogan said. "Do I get to ride around on the prince's shoulder like you do if I take you up on the offer?"

Thundar nodded. "Sure, of course."

"No, you don't." Gerald glanced over at the bar. "Anything more we should know that you haven't told us yet?"

"Them weapons you fellows are carrying are about to become illegal right quick. That's the other new law coming into effect at the end of the month. Everybody needs to turn in their swords and bows and whatever other weapons they have. Only the Emperor's men are to be armed."

Gerald blinked. "This law is supposed to apply everywhere in the Empire? Even in North Bogsonia?"

"Never heard of the place, but if it's within the boundaries of the Empire, then the law applies there as well."

Rogan laughed. "What are we supposed to do? Slay swamp pinchers with our bare hands?"

"Can this be for real?" Gerald said. "Surely these new laws are naught but foul rumors?"

"It's real enough," the barkeep said. "Proclamations have been posted all over town. That brings up another change. As of last week, public criticism of the Emperor or his policies are considered acts of treason punishable by death."

"A heck of a time to come," Gerald said.

Chapter Eighteen

Pug crept down the utility corridor.

The memory of Katja weighed heavily on his thoughts. The more he dwelled over the circumstances regarding her desperate situation, the stronger his indignation grew toward Zirac. A spirited and noble lady should have been treated with respect and honor, not used up like a cheap tool and thrown away, let alone framed for the crimes of someone else, left holding the bag while the responsible magician cackled with glee.

A shaft of light illuminated the corridor at the peephole leading to Zirac's chamber. Pug paused at the edge of the opening. Multiple voices murmured on the other side. One speaker's tone was as evil as it was distinct.

"Despite some delays, all goes as planned," Zirac said. "My minion has instructions to bring them through the pass."

A pause.

"Speak freely, worry not," Zirac said. "A few days ago, I cast a spell of silence in this room and reinforced it earlier this evening. Not even a fly on the wall can hear your words."

"You are so confident?"

"As surely as the sun rises. You doubt my abilities?"

Despite the danger, Pug smiled. What was causing Zirac to miscast his spells?

"Just so long as you aren't tripped up by a traitor among your own people," came the answer.

Pug did not recognize the identity of the second speaker. He pressed his ear against the opening in the stone wall.

"Few among the living are in a position to do me harm," Zirac said. "That old fool of an Emperor is so afraid of his own shadow that he'd willingly bathe in the jakes if I told him it'd increase his chances of survival. He won't listen to slander about the one man who already saved his life."

"A fortuitous position to be in. Does the general population support the weapon ban? They must be effectively disarmed for the plan to work. There is no chance otherwise."

"Who cares about the opinion of those fools? When the law comes into effect, then that's the law. Compliance will not be requested but enforced, and with an iron fist. The army will initiate the first large roundup of dissidents shortly thereafter."

"And the catastrophe of the Crazy Wars can be undone at long last."

"The dawn of a new day," Zirac said.

"You are so sure the citizens will allow the overthrow of their beloved Emperor, despite their being unarmed?"

"I will cut his throat myself," Zirac replied. "With their permission, if not their blessing. After all, once the supposedly invincible Empire is overrun by ogre armies, and after only a few days of fighting at that, who will dare defend the man responsible for the catastrophe?"

"Who is next on your list?"

"Councilor Jones," Zirac said. "He is a boyhood friend of the Emperor, and holds much sway among the advisors. He's also a staunch opponent of the weapon ban."

"He should go next then."

"It's all set up." Zirac cackled. "I cannot fail now."

Pug crept back from the wall, his mind whirling. Cut the Emperor's throat? Ogres overrunning the Empire? Who did he dare tell?

Chapter Nineteen

The soldiers behind the barricade frowned in unison.

"State your name and business," said one.

"I am Prince Gerald of North Bogsonia, Prince of the Marshlands, here to pay my respects to the Emperor on his upcoming birthday."

The speaker turned to a soldier at his side. "Check his name against the terrorist checklist." He turned back. "Are you expected?"

Gerald nodded. "In a sense. We received word back home that all citizens of the Empire are invited to attend the celebration."

"Things change," the soldier said. "Just the five of you in your party? Not much of a troupe for a prince."

"It was a long journey. We had to leave a few people behind along the way."

"He's not on the list," the other soldier said.

The first soldier nodded. "You may proceed about your business. The Emperor's birthday celebration takes place in three days hence. Report your arrival to the castle as soon as possible. Make sure to mention to the duty guard that you're an official representative of the homeland of yours, otherwise you'll have no chance of getting within a mile of the castle." He paused. "What's that thing on your shoulder?"

"A dragon."

"Is it dangerous?"

"Only to his enemies."

The guard grinned. "That's the way it should be. You may go about your business."

Compared to many smaller towns, where homes and security walls left streets a maze of dead ends and made through traffic impossible, Empire City was a model of organization and planning. A wide road cut a path directly through the center of the metropolis.

Side streets branched off a regular intervals, leading to shops, warehouses, and rows upon rows of three-story and four-story apartment buildings. An engraved sign above the entrance of each business announced the goods or services offered within. Symbols of drinking mugs, weapons, stars and moons, and dice seemed the most common.

Vendors occupied empty lots and alley fronts. Merchants hollered a nonstop discord. Queer beasts such as donkeys, cows, and horses shared the road with their human handlers. Luxurious palanquins swayed high above the crowds, held aloft by teams of porters. Grim-faced fighting men strutted past servants and children at play.

Gerald found himself staring every time they passed by a multistory apartment complex. The design was entirely unknown in Bogwood, yet among the most common of structures in Empire City. Some buildings shone white with a dazzling limestone finish, the main entrances decorated with hanging plants and potted flowers and protected by an armed guard. Others were little more than dilapidated hovels, the mismatched upper floors seemingly added as an afterthought. Whether rich or poor, cordage strung between the buildings supported blankets, garments, and other washables.

Even Gerald's sophisticated upbringing as a socialite in Bogwood high society had scarcely prepared his senses for the reality of Empire City. The surging masses of citizens, the smells, the shouting, and the barely restrained insanity all contributed to a general sense of chaos that seemed impossible to maintain on a daily basis. Yet here it was all the same.

"Not much like home," Parrot commented.

"I was just thinking the same thing," Gerald said.

"That's six pubs we've passed by already this morning," Rogan said.

"Later," Gerald answered. "I have business to take care of today before I get sidetracked."

"I like the way you tell people I'm dangerous," Thundar said. "I can see how you'd make a wise ruler, Gerald."

Gerald smiled. "I'm never going to get the chance to be a ruler, but I appreciate your confidence." He glanced over at Parrot. "Did you hear what he said?"

"Yes, yes, duly noted."

"Where to if not a pub?" Rogan asked.

Gerald indicated a storefront sign embossed with the image of a hammer and a hand saw surrounded by some incomprehensible scrawl. "Maybe here?"

Parrot nodded. "A good choice. Ashton Carvings reads the printed portion of the sign."

"I might as well take care of this now," Gerald said. "I'm going to duck in here for a moment."

He pushed through the front door and walked inside the shop. Chimes rang above the door. Sculptures and carving of various sizes littered the shelves along the walls. A balding, middle-aged man stood behind a desk at the far end of the room, his lips pursed, eyes narrowed, by all appearances displeased by the arrival of a potential customer.

"Is there a problem?" Gerald said.

"That thing on your shoulder . . . ."

"He's a dragon, so don't make him angry. I wish to solicit a bust of the noble King Gerald V of North Bogsonia, Lord of the Marshlands, and to take delivery as soon as possible. How long?"

"King of where?"

"North Bogsonia, the Jewel of the Empire." Gerald nodded. "King Gerald V. Do you have any of him in stock at the moment?"

The merchant laughed. "In stock? No, I can say with certainty that I do not have any King Geralds in stock at the present time."

"How long to make one up? What's your best time?"

The merchant shrugged. "Probably have it ready tomorrow, if I get busy."

"So soon?"

"Sure, I keep a good assortment of blanks in the back. A blank's a head without the finer features carved into it. You give me a description of what this king looks like, and I'll take care of the rest."

"King Gerald looks a fair bit like I do," Gerald said. "Except that he's older, with gray hair and a fair gut."

"What gut? I'm carving a bust. That's the head and shoulders."

"Right. My liege's face is a little weatherbeaten admittedly, his cheeks a tad puffy, but his eyes are rife with wisdom."

The merchant tapped a finger against the side of his head. "With your blessing, I won't include that puffy part. Experience has taught me that it's best the subject be portrayed in a more charitable light than reality might wholly warrant. Saves hurt feelings by not making the bust resemble a gargoyle."

"I see."

"It'll look great. Trust me."

Chapter Twenty

Zirac stared down on Empire City.

Decades of planning were coming to fruition at long last. Accomplishment filled his chest with a sensation akin to bursting. How long the journey had been.

As a youngster, often on the run from authorities, on countless occasions accused of being a thief by people stupid enough to leave their possessions sitting around in plain sight, a single idea even then kept his spirit strong, despite suffering through the indignity of repeated incarcerations: that there would come a day when he would be in charge. And with it, there would be a reckoning.

Who would be included among the first purge? Which group posed the greatest threat to his new order? The elder sorcerers in Wizardhome seemed the obvious first choice. Few if any magic users could conceivably rival his power in the Arts, but why take any chances? Next, he would carry out a series of more general purges among the population at large, targeting first and foremost the educated classes, the teachers, lawmakers, engineers, librarians, anyone that might conceivably prove a complication to the eternal continuity of his benevolent rule.

The waif's telepathic message cut through his revere.

"A man has arrived. He requests an audience."

Zirac stepped back from the open window. "Send him on in."

The newcomer did not even so much as glance around as he clomped up the last steps leading to the uppermost floor of the tower and came to a stop in front of Zirac's desk.

"Joe, my friend," Zirac said. "You look troubled. What ails you?"

"Bad news. Your plan to bring that advance party of ogres up through the pass has been foiled."

"What?" Zirac shouted. "Foiled how?"

"They were wiped out in Bandit," the man said. "Nothing could be done by the time I arrived. Your contact there was discovered, and the townsfolk were waiting in ambush when the ogres put ashore."

"That stupid goblin. He was told to stay quiet and keep low."

"He didn't do a very good job of it. He and some pet bug of his started eating the locals."

Zirac pressed the knuckles of his right hand against his forehead.

"You know all this for certain?"

The man nodded. "The decapitated heads of dozens of ogres decorate the waterfront in Bandit as we speak, their snarling faces basking in the sun. The head of a single goblin is there as well, along with something else I couldn't identify. Some sort of bug. Probably the one they were talking about."

"Could it get any worse?" Zirac said.

"The one piece of good news is the townsfolk seem to think that the ogres were a mere raiding party. A man I talked to in a pub was entirely convinced they had put down a rogue band looking for captives to sell as slaves in Smash. He made no mention of your greater plan, and seemed totally ignorant of the ogres' true destination."

"A shame," Zirac said.

"A significant loss, but surely they can be replaced."

"Who?" Zirac snarled. "The ogres? You think I care about them? It's the loss of time that is an insufferable affront, not to mention the necessity of setting up a different rendezvous point, as the hillbillies in Bandit are bound to be on high alert for the foreseeable future. The loss of the ogres is nothing. Why, if doing so wouldn't have tipped off the Empire and entirely ruined our plans, I'd have had half a mind to send that first group on a rampage through the streets of Empire City. My, but what a scandal that would have caused! They wouldn't have lasted long of course, soldiers would put them to the sword in short order, but even the mere sight of a pillaging ogre would frighten ten years off the average citizen's lifespan."

"The champion who killed your property and upset your plans is visiting Empire City at this very moment, if you'd like to have words with him over the matter."

Zirac stood up. "You should have said something earlier. Who is this champion? From where does he slither?"

"He's but a soldier in the company of one Prince Gerald of North Bogsonia."

Zirac sneered. "A swamp pig? You can't be serious."

"A guard on duty reported their arrival earlier today."

"How convenient. None of them shall leave the city alive."

Chapter Twenty-One

Royal Castle glistened like a jewel in the afternoon sun.

"We'll, I'll be an eagle." Thundar said. "What a place."

Thick stone walls studded with towers and observation posts surrounded the perimeter of the estate, but in every real sense, luxury had replaced function. There remained no sign of the portcullis that would have sealed shut the main gates during an attack. The mote surrounding the castle contained only sand. Rooftops glistened under golden tiles and windowsills sparkled in silver splendor, materials too soft for use in any sort of working military citadel.

Soldiers manned a roadblock at the entrance to the Imperial Grounds.

"State your name and business," said one.

"I am Gerald, Prince of the Marshlands, third in line to the crown of North Bogsonia, the Jewel of the Empire. I have arrived to pay my respects to the Emperor on the event of his upcoming birthday."

"You're the ones from the swamp?"

Gerald's face went momentarily slack. "You heard we were coming? North Bogsonia is a beautiful land of course but—"

"Come with me," the guard said.

Thundar maintained his most stately facial expression as Gerald and the rest of the company followed the guard through the remaining checkpoints before the castle. A few words from their escort at each station proved sufficient to continue on. Guards eyed Rogan and his axe with thinly veiled suspicion.

A paved walkway led to the castle entrance. A pair of oversized doors opened into a lobby decorated with rare woods, exotic metals, and minutely detailed statues. In the center of the room, a fountain spouted an endless stream of water from the mouth of a carved stone lion. Tapestries embroidered with intricate patterns decorated the walls. A second set of doors, fabulously decorated in gold sheeting and etched with glyphs of dragons, soldiers, griffons, trolls, and other creatures provided an entryway into a cavernous throne room.

Gold and silver sparkled. Chandeliers hung from the frescoed ceiling, dangling in the air like a sadistic trap, a serious hazard for any flying creature, especially a dragon, but pretty all the same. Never before during Thundar's entire lifetime, a span of years that encompassed nearly an entire decade, had he witnessed the like. Statues and sculptures and incomprehensible paintings, each one likely the creation of a human master, lined the walls. Jewels glittered. Tiles shimmered.

"That wood carving of your father's head will really add some zest to this place. Give it some class."

"Quiet."

A tiered dais dominated the throne room. An old man sat upon a golden throne in the center of the uppermost level of the dais. Slate gray hair hung nearly to his shoulders. The flesh beneath his eyes sagged.

A crowd of servants stood directly behind the throne. A strikingly beautiful young woman occupied a chair at the Emperor's side. Golden tresses spiraled down her shoulders. On the Emperor's opposite side sat a thin, evil-looking magician, distinctive in his black robes. Thundar disliked the man on sight.

The magician's face remained hidden behind a large hood, shaded from view other than a long, curving nose that jutted out from his face like the beak of a vulture, and a pair of mustard yellow eyes. A faint scent of decay clung to his skin—or to his robes—with an unmistakable foulness, reeking all the way across the room. As if reading Thundar's thoughts, the magician glared down from the dais, his flat gaze disdainful, mouth pursed in a pinch.

A crier hollered Gerald's name. Everyone on the dais, including the Emperor, stopped what they were doing and stared down on Gerald and his party. A servant rushed up to the throne and spoke with the Emperor.

"Welcome to Empire City." The Emperor spoke slowly. "You who serve the Empire are welcome."

Gerald smiled. "The citizens of North Bogsonia live to serve the Empire. We are but thy humble servants."

"I wish only that all my subjects were so devoted."

"Be it true that you are the ones who killed the ghoul?" said the woman beside the Emperor.

"A few introductions are in order," the Emperor said. "This is my daughter, the Lady Gwendolyn, with whom you have the privilege of speaking. This gentleman is my trusted advisor, Zirac. My daughter refers to an incident in the town of Bandit that you are reported to have participated."

"My man, Rogan, he is the hero," Gerald said. "Rogan the Axe Slayer volunteered to slay the monster despite the scores of warriors that had already died in the attempt."

"Those men that died were fishermen," Zirac said. "Spare us your tall tales."

"Now, now," the Emperor said. "Gwendolyn asked our guest to comment on the affair, and I am interested in hearing about it myself. Now, which one of you men is Rogan?"

Rogan stepped forward.

"You are the slayer of the ghoul?" the Emperor asked.

"I am, though men called the creature a god at the time."

"And a goblin? A goblin was this creature's handler? You slew it as well?"

"I did."

"One small goblin is hardly—" Zirac began.

The Emperor waved his hand. "A single dead goblin or a thousand, each is a contribution."

"Prince Gerald," the woman called down. "You and your men have served the Empire well. You are a credit to your land."

Gerald smiled.

"My personal thanks to you, Axe Slayer, for a job well done," the Emperor said.

"I was glad to do it."

"And as for you, Prince Gerald," the Emperor said. "We heard word regarding the labors that you and your people took to reach our fair city in time for our little celebration. Such sacrifice, and all in the hopes of doing your beloved Emperor an honor. Your dedication is an example to all citizens and speaks volumes regarding your loyalty to the Crown."

Gerald nodded and smiled.

"Prince Gerald is hereby designated an official hero of the Empire," the Emperor announced. "As such, my young friend, your presence will be expected at my party."

"My thanks, Sire."

Zirac glowered.

Chapter Twenty-Two

The streets of Empire City swarmed with traffic. Banners and ribbons and flower petals and tissue paper decorated lamp posts and storefronts and street signs. Pennons fluttered from laundry lines suspended high above the ground. Crowds packed the pubs and gaming houses.

Thundar held on tight to Gerald's shoulder as they wrestled their way through the masses of humanity.

"The Emperor sure was impressed by Rogan slaying that evil dog," he said.

"That was an evil god, you chicken," Rogan said. "And the mixup wasn't my doing."

"Sad how some people can't let things go," Parrot said.

"What about food?" Red asked. "I'm hungry. Hungry for ale."

Skunk shook his head. "Starving is more like it. Starving for grog."

"You two go ahead," Gerald said. "Rogan, Parrot, join them if you wish."

"Where are you off to?" Rogan asked.

"I must pick up the Emperor's gift from the woodworker. The party is tonight, and the woodcarver said the bust would be ready."

"Finally," Thundar said. "Something elegant in the castle."

"I heard you the first time," Gerald said.

"A gift of dubious taste is immeasurably better than no gift at all," Parrot said. "To arrive at the Emperor's party empty handed would be a taken as a sign of disrespect."

"There's nothing dubious about the bust," Gerald said. "It'll be great, trust me."

"I think the Emperor likes you," Thundar said. "But the muscles in your shoulder tensed up as hard as a rock when you were staring at that sorcerer."

"Was it that obvious? He was giving me a glare, so I returned the favor. I wonder why he even took special notice of us? Visitors must enter the throne room all the time."

Thundar shrugged. "Maybe nobody else even noticed you two staring. I was standing on your shoulder and so had a closer view of the whole thing than most."

"I noticed," said Rogan.

"So did I," Skunk agreed.

Red spoke from the back of the group. "He wanted to do you harm, prince."

"Why would the Emperor allow such a man in his court?" Gerald asked.

"It's the result of the Crazy Wars," Parrot explained. "In order to placate the sorcerers following their defeat, the Emperor agreed to allow a single mage to sit on his council of advisors."

Rogan turned to Thundar. "Your cousins chose the wrong side during that little skirmish."

Thundar nodded. "Best never to get involved in politics, that's the lesson there. But dragons fought on both sides during the Crazy Wars."

"He's right," Parrot said. "While all major species of dragons were wiped out by the end of the conflict, extinct along with the dwarves and elves, and most did side with the ogres and goblins, some chose to fight alongside man. They all paid the ultimate price in the end."

"A terrible tragedy, just awful," Thundar said. "Unbelievably bad. The extinction of the major dragon lines is the single greatest catastrophe in the history of the universe, bar none. No other event in memory is so gut-wrenching and horrible, no loss so evil—"

"That probably depends on who you're talking to," Gerald said. "And on the species of the person you ask. Anyhow, here's the woodcarver's shop. Thundar, do you wish to join them for ale or are you staying with me?"

"I'll stay with you," Thundar said. "The smoke in a pub makes the insides of my chest itch. Dragons like clean air. It probably comes from soaring among the clouds."

Rogan snorted. "You ride atop the prince's shoulder every chance you get. You're about three times the size as when you first crashed in front of us. Look at you, you're even getting a swag belly."

Thundar placed his hands across his stomach. "Do you really think I'm getting plump? Imagine that. If only that ungrateful wretch of a mate of mine could see me now. How jealous she'd be. Growing plump indeed!"

"I didn't mean it as a compliment," Rogan said.

"Rogan's right," Gerald said. "You're a lot more dragon to pack around now than when we first met. You should try to get a little more exercise and cut back on the desserts. You won't be able to fly at all before long if you keep gaining weight."

"He can just roll around from place to place like a ball of scales." Rogan laughed.

"I thought we were going to the woodcarver's shop," Thundar said. "Speaking of a wooden head."

Gerald nodded. "So we are."

"Come, chronicler," Rogan said. "Come along and test your liver with fighting men."

"Have a good time." Gerald veered into the woodcarver's shop, forcing Thundar to duck beneath the doorsill else be knocked from his perch.

The door chimes jingled and the merchant waved from behind the desk.

"Welcome back, young prince. Your order was ready yesterday, as promised."

"I waited an extra day because I wanted to not rush you," Gerald said. "And I did not need the piece until today."

The woodcarver smiled. "Your faith in Ashton Carvings is well rewarded. I am positive you will be thrilled with the results. Allow me but a moment."

Thundar waited impatiently as the woodcarver retreated to a back room.

"Are you excited, Gerald?"

"About what? The party?"

"No, the gift. I'll bet it impresses the Emperor."

The woodcarver returned, a bulky object in his hands hidden under a piece of cloth.

"Observe and shout for joy." The woodcarver tore away the cloth with a flourish.

"It looks just like you, Gerald," Thundar said.

Gerald's jaw dropped open. "But it looks just like me."

The woodcarver grinned. "As promised, a slightly younger version of King Gerald V, am I right? You said this man is your father?"

"Yes, but . . . ." Gerald pointed. "The Emperor will think I'm giving him a bust of myself."

"You'll look like a fool," Thundar said.

"Yes, quite the fool. Woodcarver, can't you age it up a little?"

The woodcarver placed his hands protectively atop the bust. "This is a work of art. It is what it is, and anything else imposed upon it is a lie. You may solicit a different work if you are unsatisfied, but you still owe me for this one."

"How much?"

"Two silvers."

"Is that all?"

The woodcarver shrugged. "Wasn't much to it, like I said, I just added the finer features to a blank."

"Pretty cheap gift for an Emperor," Thundar said. "Put the cloth back over it."

Gerald carried the bust outside and they continued down the street.

Thundar shook his head. "On the bright side, that bust cost less than would have that keg of ale the boys wanted to get instead. I don't know if it's the best gift the Emperor has ever received, but it's almost certainly the thriftiest."

"I didn't get it because it's cheap," Gerald said. "The image of the king of North Bogsonia represents the people of North Bogsonia. Besides, I didn't have any choice but to take it. The party is tonight, remember?"

"Maybe the Emperor won't even notice what you got him," Thundar said. "He must receive hundreds of presents each year, thousands maybe. He can't possibly keep track of who gives him what."

"I hope you're right," Gerald said. "I'll just slip this bust among the other gifts when we get to the palace. With luck, nobody will even see us."

Chapter Twenty-Three

"You want to know what the problem is with people?" Zirac said. "People are idiots, that's the problem. You should have seen Gwendolyn gawking at that swamp monkey. Batting her eyelids like some kind of a moron. Smiling like a fool. Just watch her pull that same nonsense tonight, all full of questions for the country rube, pretending to seek his advice on one retarded subject after another. I've been in the throne room for years and not once has she spoken to me. Never even looked in my direction. How's that for intelligent?"

The waif hovered without comment.

"What did you say?" Zirac said.

"The man you sent for has arrived."

"Bring him here."

The waif floated from the room. Zirac dropped into his chair and sighed. The claw in the jar tapped a steady beat against its glass home, but Zirac was too preoccupied to enjoy even that spectacle. Had he miscalculated? His latest bit of manipulation seemed so subtly ingenious at the time. By anonymously putting into circulation a story extolling the heroics of the laughable Prince Gerald, heaping praise on the Bogsonian fools for their bumblings in Bandit, he had fixed it so that they would be assured a seat at the table of the most prominent members of the court, and therefore available to be implicated as the guilty party in the unfortunate passing of the doomed Councilor Jones.

But who could have foreseen the reaction of the Princess Gwendolyn to the presence of the Bogsonian prince? She was taking entirely too much interest in the slow-witted hick, despite his egregious inferiorities to the suave—not to mention readily available—magician directly in front of her eyes. Women were mysterious creatures indeed.

The mere thought of the other loose end still to be dealt with filled him with irritation in an instant. The harlot of a woman, Katja, remained at large despite his best efforts to have her captured. Scores of guards and trained trackers were as yet unable to pick up the woman's trail. It was almost as if she had disappeared off the face of the earth.

He took a deep breath and exhaled slowly. Katja was not a real threat to his power, he reminded himself, and there remained only so many places to hide in the Empire. They would catch her eventually.

The waif returned to the inner chamber trailed by a portly man man in a plain white tunic. The newcomer's head and face remained obscured within the folds of a voluminous hood, a most becoming style, Zirac noted.

"Thanks for coming, Jack." Zirac used his warm, friendly tone. "How are you tonight, my old friend?"

"You sent for me?" The man gazed nervously in the direction of the waif.

Zirac suppressed a giggle at the other's discomfort.

"Why are you all covered up, Jack?"

Jack pushed back his hood. His dark hair shone with sweat.

"I can't be seen anywhere near you, Zirac. I cook the Emperor's food for the sake of—"

"Calm down," Zirac said. "You'll give yourself away acting so nervous. Your hands are shaking."

The other man grew completely still. "Why did you send for me?"

"What you mean to say is what do I want this time? Why don't I hurry up and get it over with? I'm beginning to think you don't value our friendship as much as I do, Jack."

"Friendship." Jack spat. "You got me off the hook that one time, and I'll repay my debt to you, but don't think I enjoy it."

"Off the hook is right," Zirac said. "What were you doing again? Oh, right, you strangled your wife and were stupid enough to get caught dumping the body. That'd get you executed if the authorities were to find out. Poor Jack."

Jack looked away.

"One last favor," Zirac said. "It's a big one, but afterwards we'll call our little arrangement even."

"Yeah?" Jack said. "Last one forever? Okay. What is it?"

"I need you to place a special powder on the roast chicken served to Councilor Jones at the banquet tonight. I know he likes his chicken cooked extremely well done, burned nearly black in fact, so there's no chance of mixing up his dish with that of any of the other guests."

"What kind of powder?"

"Oh, a special kind. It's guaranteed to take away all his problems."

Jack blanched. "More poison? I'm the cook, Zirac. They'll know I'm the one that did it. They'll torture me until I speak."

"Have no fear. The blame is going on another. There's no danger, not to you. It'll all go off great."

"What about the food tasters?" Jack said. "Remember them? I doubt Councilor Jones will still want his meal after the taster that tries it keels over and dies."

"The taster will receive an antidote for the poison before the meal is served."

"Think for a moment," Jack said. "The tasters are assigned to guests at random. They don't even know themselves whose food it is they're tasting. How can you be sure to give the antidote to the right person?"

"I can't," Zirac admitted. "Which is why the antidote will be served to the entire staff before the banquet begins. None of the servants will so much as raise an eyebrow when you call for a toast to honor the Emperor's birthday, a tribute served from a bottle of wine that I have prepared special for the occasion. Antidote wine, you might say."

Jack rubbed his jaw. His right eye twitched. "That might work. Alright, but after this, we're even forever."

"Of course." Zirac forced a smile to his lips. "You have my word. Trust me."

Chapter Twenty-Four

Thundar held on tight to Gerald's shoulder as they dodged around a donkey cart.

"You new tunic looks really slick, Gerald, all shiny and purple. It makes you look like a prince."

"I am a prince," Gerald said.

"So it's fitting you wear something that makes you look the part, that's my point. You smell like you've had a bath as well."

"It was time," Gerald said. "Probably past time, but better late than never."

Thundar glanced back over his shoulder. The setting sun lit up the western horizon in a red glow. The Emperor's party would begin shortly.

"We're going to be late. I don't want to have to spur my mount. Giddy up."

"Don't you dare. We have plenty of time. Relax."

Gerald fumbled with the bust as he walked, switching the load from one arm to the other. A long, steep hill left the prince puffing like a man twice his age.

"You need to lose some weight," Gerald joked. "Or start flying. Between this bust and the overweight dragon on my shoulder, my arms are going numb."

"You'll make it, you're young," Thundar encouraged. "And you're probably unaware of the fact that a large belly is considered a sign of wealth and beauty among my kind."

"No wonder sailors choose parrots for their mascots. Birds are light."

"Birds," Thundar scoffed. Twin jets of flame shot from his nostrils. "Birds only mimic the speech of more intelligent creatures. They don't actually understand the words that come out of their mouths. But parrots do taste a lot like chicken, I'll give them that. No, you want a dragon if you're looking for good company and intelligent conversation, a red dragon to be specific."

Gerald dodged around another cart.

"Shouldn't we be traveling with a big retinue and guards and the whole bit?" Thundar asked. "We're a royal procession after all, en route to the Emperor's birthday party. Attending by special invite no less. You're a hero. The Emperor even said so."

"I suppose we might have requested an honor guard," Gerald said. "Though it never dawned on me until now. I know how to find my way to the castle. A man should do a thing for himself if he can."

"You don't talk very much like a royal person, Gerald. You'll probably grow out of it sooner or later."

Gerald grinned. "People are accustomed to doing things for themselves in North Bogsonia. I don't mean my father, he has lots of help. I'm talking about the average person. We don't have servants to do every little thing back home."

"Not even you?" Thundar said. "A prince?"

Gerald shrugged. "Okay, I have a lot of servants as well, but again, I'm royalty. What I'm saying is that there's no indentured servants among the average folk."

"That's wise, they'd just get lazy." Thundar rubbed his belly. "In this uncertain age, we all need to keep on our toes. Does Empire City hold no interest for you?"

"It's just so much different than in Bogwood. I give these city folks credit for that. There's always something going on around here, even in the middle of the night. There's no exaggeration in the expression that the city never sleeps."

"Dedicated to noise is what they are," Thundar said.

"I wouldn't want to live here, not for the long haul. The air is dry, the streets are dusty and crowded with people. It'd get on my nerves before long."

Thundar nodded. "Limited hunting opportunities as well. An unemployed dragon could starve in this city. There's not a pheasant or a rabbit in the entire area. Maybe I could sing in a pub for cash."

"You sing?"

"Not very well, but working as an entertainer would beat snatching food from a garbage pail any day."

"I thought dragons are supposed to be predators? Rather than scavengers?"

"We are, but again, there has to be something to catch. And for the record, what you don't want to do under any circumstances is snatch a little old lady's dog, no matter how hungry you are. Bound to get the entire population of a whole town chasing you, all of them trying to fill your backside with arrows. Trust me, I know."

"You're a long way from starvation now," Gerald observed. "I can't believe the weight of you."

"It's not too much farther to the palace from here," Thundar encouraged. "You can do it, you're so strong."

"Can't you flap your wings and help us along, even carry us up to the palace?"

"The force of the updraft would rip your shoulder off," Thundar said. "Sorry."

"I'll bet."

They crested a hill.

"Do you like the Princess Gwendolyn?" Thundar asked.

"What?"

"Do you like her? Because she was staring at you in the throne room earlier, but in a different way than Zirac was staring. If the two of you end up together, you'll need to move to Empire City to satisfy her father, the Emperor."

Gerald laughed. "I know who Gwendolyn's father is, and he's not about to marry his precious little girl off to the likes of myself."

"Oh," Thundar said. "Human relationships are complex."

"Especially to the humans involved," Gerald agreed.

Guards in full dress uniform manned the checkpoints leading to the castle. Resplendent in red tunics and shiny helms, the addition of purple cloaks added an air of sophistication to their appearance that left Thundar nodding in appreciation.

Despite Gerald's assurances to the contrary, the party proved to be already in full swing. Men and women garbed in shimmering attire crowded the throne room and the hallway beyond. Thundar felt suddenly underdressed for the occasion. He pulled down on his helm and straightened his cloak.

The tiered dais where the Emperor sat remained the sole area free of revelers. An unbroken line of soldiers stood at the base of the platform. Of the Emperor and his staff, there was no sign.

Off to the side of the throne room, a mound of gaily wrapped packages in an array of shapes and colors loaded down a low table.

"Are those the gifts for the Emperor over there?"

"Looks that way." Gerald held up the bust. "I'll be glad to get rid of this thing."

Thundar clamped his feet tightly to Gerald's shoulder as they moved through the crowd. Dancing guests swung their arms about with abandon, repeatedly forcing Thundar to duck to avoid being struck. A wayward forearm rebounded off the side of Gerald's head with an audible slap. Unable to defend himself due to the bust in his hands, the prince cursed a blue streak.

A chorus of brass horns erupted in a blast of earsplitting noise. The party came to a stop. Dancers went still. The musicians made not another note. A court crier in a crimson tunic walked out to the center of the throne room. He lifted his arms overhead.

"Ladies and gentlemen, your attention please. I have the pleasure of introducing the person responsible for our gathering this evening."

Applause. The crier shushed the crowd with a wave.

"As you all know, that most cherished event of the year is upon us at long last. The Emperor's birthday has arrived."

Loud applause. The crier held up his hands.

"Despite some recent unpleasantness at court and elsewhere, every citizen of the Empire can be sure that our guest of honor has lost none of his enthusiasm for this great event. So without further ado, here he is, our beloved Emperor."

The Emperor and the Princess Gwendolyn made their appearance to an eruption of hoots and applause. A retinue of guards followed on their heels. The Emperor looked exhausted. He walked in a stoop. The princess, smiling and radiant, carried a small, odd-smelling animal nested in the crook of her arm. The species was new in Thundar's experience. Despite the onset of the summer season, the creature retained a white winter fur coat, a perfect camouflage for hunting over snowdrifts but a dead giveaway among the browns and greens of a lush forest.

"What's that thing she's carrying? What is it?"

"The cat?" Gerald said.

"That furry thing. About the right size for a meal."

"Don't you dare. It's a cat, and you cannot eat it. Not even if it provokes you, understand? Don't touch it. Not ever. I mean it."

"Okay, of course I won't eat it. Obviously."

"You were licking your lips."

"They were dry," Thundar protested. "You try having a kiln in your chest."

Partygoers cheered frenziedly. Thundar nearly added a blast of dragonfire to the general hoopla but reconsidered due to the risk of setting a blaze among the banners and tapestries fastened along the ceiling. He let loose with a traditional dragon call instead, a drawn-out screech of strength and defiance, a challenge from the shadowy mists of time. Partygoers turned and stared, undoubtedly impressed.

The crowd parted like a wave in front of the Emperor. Thundar found he was increasingly squished against Gerald's head in the press of the mob, in moments unable to so much as move a wing if he tried.

The Emperor walked past only a few paces distant. Much to Thundar's surprise, the princess came to a stop directly in front of Gerald.

"Doesn't he look fierce?" Gwendolyn pointed at Gerald and laughed. "I love the way that chubby little dragon wears his cute little helmet and cape everywhere. It's just too funny."

Thundar nearly fell to the floor in surprise: despite the Lady Gwendolyn's great physical beauty, she sounded naive. Foolish, even.

The Emperor's mouth lifted in a smile. "The Bogsonian and his dragon, is it? How are you doing tonight, young man?"

"I am fine, Sire. And yourself and the Lady Gwendolyn?"

Thundar looked around. Nearly everyone at the party stared their way, expectant looks on their faces. Other than the voices of the Emperor and Gerald, the throne room was silent.

"We're both good." The Emperor pointed. "What have you got in your hands?"

"Oh." Gerald held the bust down by his waist. "This. It's nothing. Just a thing I was going to put with the other gifts."

"It's a gift for me?"

"Yes, Sire."

The Emperor chuckled. "Isn't this nice? I haven't even made it to my throne yet, and already the presents are coming in. Okay, let's have it."

"Sire?"

"My gift, let's have it." The Emperor lifted his arms. "The first gift I shall open this year will be the one from my friends from North Bogsonia."

Murmurs rippled through the crowd. Partygoers smiled and clapped their hands.

"I can just put it over there with the others," Gerald suggested.

"Nonsense," the Emperor said. "I'll open it right here and now. I must admit, I'm more than a little curious to see what my subjects from your far realm brought me."

Gerald passed his gift to the Emperor. Guests crowded close, heedless of proper etiquette. Gwendolyn smiled beautifully. Even a few members of the Emperor's personal guard forgot their place and glanced back toward their charge rather than properly study the crowd.

The Emperor tore away the cloth from the bust, revealing the wood carving underneath. The smile on his face never wavered.

"A bust of . . . yourself, young prince?"

Gwendolyn frowned. The guards flushed. A woman somewhere in the crowd giggled. Thundar fought against a sudden instinct to cover his eyes with a wing in embarrassment.

"Oh, and what's this?" The Emperor turned the bust over, revealing the underside. "Made locally by one Ashton Carvings."

"The bust is but an image of my father, King Gerald V," Gerald said. "The gift my father intended for you to have was lost on our journey hither, in a shipwreck as we entered the bay at Bandit. That was before my man, Rogan, defeated the monster terrifying the villagers and destroyed its goblin handler."

An approving babble swept the crowd. Gwendolyn recovered her smile. The expressions of the guards softened.

"Yes, that goblin business was well done," the Emperor said. "The incident has gained a certain folklore status already. If only all my subjects were so loyal."

Gerald spoke in a low tone. "The bust was all that we had time to get you before the party."

"Yes, yes, the gift doesn't matter. In fact, I like it a lot." The Emperor lifted the bust in his arms. "I hereby decree that this magnificent gift from North Bogsonia be placed atop the mantle in my favorite sleeping quarters."

The crowd erupted in cheers. Gerald nodded both to his left and right as guests on all sides shouted compliments and congratulations. Thundar coolly acknowledged their admiration with slight nods of his head.

"My thanks, Sire," Gerald said.

The Lady Gwendolyn whispered in the ear of the Emperor. The monarch nodded. A wisp of a smile crossed his features.

"Prince Gerald, you will join us at my personal table for the feast this evening. As my honored guest."

Chapter Twenty-Five

Thundar stared at the polished utensils atop the table, the gem encrusted spice shakers, the condiment dispensers, the crystal mugs and silver plates, each item worth a small fortune. Shiny and attractive. Treasure by any dragon's standards.

"I wish my armor had some pockets. Just look at all this stuff."

"Don't you dare," Gerald said.

Thundar leaned back against his plush seat at the royal table. About a dozen servants hovered over the Emperor and Gwendolyn, but food for the guests was yet to be seen. Several seats down from the Emperor, the dark from of Zirac sat in a stooped hump, the black hood covering his head so that only his long nose remained visible.

"Why does the mage not wear jewels as these others?" Thundar asked.

"The nobles display their wealth because it is the source of their power," Gerald said. "Zirac's strength stems from a different origin."

"Speaking of keeping up one's strength," Thundar said, "when are they serving dinner around here? I'm famished."

"Pretty soon. Be patient."

Guests continued to arrive. In short order, the huge banquet room was filled to capacity. Thundar kept a sharp eye out for any sign of the promised food. So far, nothing. He shook his head: what was the point of tempting guests with the promise of a nice meal, only to turn around and refuse to serve the food in a timely manner? Was it all some kind of sick joke?

"What kind of an animal is that at your side, sir?" said a man seated two places down.

"A red dragon," Gerald said.

"Really? I say. Is she about to give birth?"

"No." Gerald grinned. "You may find this hard to believe, but Thundar is actually a male dragon. He's just been eating a little too well lately."

Thundar considered giving both men a dose of flames.

"He's been eating a lot too well from the looks of it," said the stranger.

"Take a look in a mirror." Thundar pointed at the man's abdomen with a claw. "Speaking of looking pregnant . . . ."

"You talk?" The man smiled. "Very impressive. Why do you wear that helmet?"

"Battle, what else? You'd understand if you were a dragon."

"Allow me to introduce myself. I am Councilor Jones, third on the council of advisors."

"And I am Prince Gerald, visiting from North Bogsonia, the Jewel of the Empire."

The councilor smiled. "Indeed. This is my wife, Sonia."

A woman seated at the councilor's far side nodded her head.

"A pleasure," Thundar said. "And I am Thundar, known as Skymaster by some."

"By some," Gerald stressed. "But as of late, Thundar has more often been called Chicken Eater, and Ale Drinker, and the like."

Thundar rubbed his belly. "Please excuse the prince's remarks, Councilor Jones. North Bogsonians are an isolated people, and their backward sense of humor takes some growing accustomed to. I hope you'll be patient."

"Not at all," Councilor Jones said. "There's a contingent here in the city from South Bogsonia as well. Your people are becoming more common in the Empire every day."

Gerald frowned. "South Bogsonians aren't my people. Where did you say they were seated?"

Councilor Jones swiveled his head back and forth and shrugged. "I don't see them right now, but they were here earlier. So they say you're the one that gave the Emperor the bust he likes so much. And solicited the piece from a local artist at that. I can only imagine the flood of orders that will pour into that particular artist's shop over the next few days. He'll never work his way out from under it all, though I suspect he'll get rich trying. Every wealthy person in the Empire will want an identical bust for their own home."

"Not only just the wealthy can afford it," Thundar said. "The bust cost but a pittance."

"Indeed?"

Thundar nodded. "Two whole silvers, not bad for impressing the Emperor. Ashton Carvings should give Gerald a cut of the profits for the free publicity."

Councilor Jones looked startled. "Two silvers?"

Gerald coughed in his hand. "I don't recall the exact amount, but the price was irrelevant. The thought behind the gift was what mattered."

"As always," the councilor said.

"Have you heard a rumor involving an impending ban on weapons, councilor?" Gerald asked.

"It's no rumor, but real," Councilor Jones said. "What is the take in your homeland on the ban?"

"I don't think anybody in North Bogsonia is aware of it. Such a law simply would not work there. The citizens would get eaten by the local animals. Without a means to defend ourselves, we would be helpless."

Councilor Jones nodded. "As will we all if this new law comes to pass. But fear not, nothing is yet written in stone, and every day brings new changes."

"The situation regarding the food seems fairly static," Thundar said. "When do people eat in this part of the world?"

"Quite soon. Too bad you're not a mage as well as dragon, else you might conjure up something to tide you over until we are served. Some dragons were renowned magic users back in the old days. You might have waved a magic wand and brought forth a cupcake to tide you over."

"No thanks," Thundar said. "Sorcerers are evil, no matter what the species, especially that smelly Zirac. If I were the Emperor, I'd banish him to Wizardhome for sure."

"Quiet, you," Gerald said.

Councilor Jones grinned. "Those are the truest words spoken in this castle for a long time. Dangerous and foolhardy words perhaps, but true all the same."

"Don't worry, Gerald can take down Zirac any time he wants," Thundar said.

"That's enough, thanks," Gerald said.

Councilor Jones smiled once again. "A little honesty around here is a nice change, like a breath of fresh air. Is there anything I can assist you gentlemen with while you visit? I've lived in this city my entire life and admittedly know it quite well."

"Is the Princess Gwendolyn betrothed to be married?" Thundar said. "I'm asking for a friend."

"No, she is not betrothed. She has not yet met a man whom she deems suitable for marriage, and her father is loath to press her into a union she opposes."

"Nobody is interested?" Thundar said. "I'm no expert, but she seems to be very pretty by human standards."

"She is the fairest woman in the land," Councilor Jones said. "And a genuinely pleasant person as well, humble and kind. No few potential suitors have made the mistake of attempting to win her approval through ostentatious displays of wealth and power, never understanding that she has been privy to such things since childhood and puts no store by them. But no matter, someone is bound to figure it out sooner or later, after all, nearly every bachelor in the Empire would give anything to have her." He nodded in the direction of Zirac. "Any man interested in a woman, that is."

A chorus of dinner chimes rang out. Teams of servants carrying huge silver platters moved into the banquet room and split up among the various tables. Thundar accepted a double helping of roast lamb along with a pair of steaming pork chops, but declined an offering of fried greens. He added a half-dozen deep fried giant crawfish to his plate, a personal favorite. His mouth watered at the mere sight of the racks of the steaming ribs, hams, and beefsteak.

"I'm going to need another plate."

"Eat what you've got first," Gerald said. "Then take more. How do you manage to put so much away anyhow?"

"Dragons have a very high metabolism. Internal kilns burn off lots of calories, not to mention the energy consumed by flying."

"But dragons that don't do either one, fly or make fire, they tend to put on a little weight . . . ." Gerald trailed off.

Thundar nodded. "Yes, I've seen it happen."

Councilor Jones flashed a smile as a servant removed a cover from a round platter and revealed a badly overcooked chicken, the skin blackened by fire. Surprisingly, the councilor reacted to the sad sight with an even wider grin.

"Looks good, doesn't it?"

Thundar preferred his own food raw or nearly so, but in the interest of politeness, he leaned over the table and took a long sniff in the air above the overcooked meat. Along with the expected scent, there came to his senses a sickly sweetness, a spice he supposed, but carrying a particularly foul odor. The lingering scent caused him to sniff at the chicken a second time and a third.

"It's that good?" Councilor Jones laughed.

"No," Thundar said. "I wouldn't eat it."

"Why not?"

"It'll make you sick or worse. There's something bad in it."

Councilor Jones shrugged. "I can't smell a thing. What do you say, Prince Gerald?"

Gerald leaned over the plate. "It does smell strange. Where do I know that scent from?" He scratched his head.

"It seems fine to me." Councilor Jones lifted a blackened chicken leg to his mouth.

Gerald jumped to his feet and grabbed the councilor's hand. "One mouthful of that and you'll be dead."

Councilor Jones dropped the chicken leg like a hot coal.

"Gravedigger," Gerald said. "That's gravedigger on your food, the smell is unmistakable. It's a fairly common sight in North Bogsonia, but I never expected to see it here, for it is a swamp nettle."

Councilor Jones sniffed at his plate."On second thought, it does smell a tad strange. I just lost my appetite." He pushed back his chair from the table. "Guards! Where are the food tasters? There is treachery afoot."

A commotion ensued. A servant in flowing white robes whispered to the Emperor. Gwendolyn frowned and crossed her arms. Guards ran to and fro. One guest after another pushed back his or her plate and stepped away from the table.

"What goes on here?" The Emperor rose to his feet. "Who says there is a problem with the food?"

"It is our guest from the swamp, Majesty," Zirac said. "Perhaps he is suffering from a bout of indigestion. Outrageous that he disturbs your feast with his nonsense."

"It is I who have the concern," Councilor Jones said. "Prince Gerald and his dragon detected something wrong with the food, and I concur. Seeing as how one of my colleagues recently met his death from a still-unsolved case of poisoning, it goes without saying that caution is in order."

"This is ridiculous," Zirac said. "Eat up, everybody."

"What's it to you, mage?" Councilor Jones said. "Sit down and keep quiet."

Zirac sighed audibly. "Sire, I object to this embarrassment at your dining table, and during your birthday feast at that. Surely this man is simply paranoid or intoxicated."

"Perhaps he is," the Emperor said. "But the councilor has a point. Considering some recent events around here, crimes in which my security people have been unable to locate the culprits responsible, people are bound to be sensitive. Bring the dish in question over here."

A servant placed the platter of blackened chicken in front of the Emperor.

"Why is this food burned?"

"That's how the councilor prefers it prepared," a servant answered.

"Is this true?" the Emperor said. "You actually like your food like this? It's ridiculous."

Councilor Jones shrugged. "Not all food do I prefer so, but the chicken I eat must be thoroughly cooked to avoid digestive problems later. But my concern is elsewhere at the moment. This young man insists there is poison in my food. I smell something as well."

"What foolishness," Zirac said. "Majesty, there is an easy way to settle this. Simply bring out a taster and have him consume a portion of that burned fowl right here in front of us. Then we can get back to dinner."

"Why bother with a food taster, Majesty?" Councilor Jones said. "Zirac is in such a rush to get back to his meal, surely he'd be willing to eat from the dish in question?"

Zirac blinked. "Magicians . . . don't eat chicken."

The Emperor frowned. "Since when? You ate a whole bird at the last banquet. I remember telling you there was a bone stuck to your hood."

"Overcooked chicken, that is," Zirac said. "The black bits are very bad for spell casting, as they interfere with energy fields and the like, unlike . . . medium well chicken."

"I see." The Emperor sounded unconvinced. "In any case, where is that taster?"

"On his way, Majesty," said a servant.

"Are you sure, Gerald?" Thundar whispered. "It couldn't be some sort of spice that only smells the same?"

Gerald shrugged.

A tomblike silence greeted the small group of food tasters as they approached the royal table. Hardly a single person so much as moved.

"I am the one who tasted that dish," said one man among the group of tasters. "I verify that I ate a portion of that burnt chicken and report no ill effects as of yet."

The Emperor pointed. "Smell it again. Tell me if it is as before."

The man complied. "So far as I can tell, it is."

"Go ahead and eat some," the Emperor said.

The servant tore into the chicken as if he hadn't eaten in a week, stuffing his face until his cheeks swelled, smacking his lips without so much as a sign of indigestion let alone poisoning.

Thundar watched with increasing embarrassment. Councilor Jones blushed red. The Emperor fidgeted with his robe. Lady Gwendolyn looked distracted and stroked the cat in her lap. Only Zirac appeared pleased, tipping back in his chair, arms crossed, a smile playing across his face.

"Really good," the food taster reported. "No sign of anything wrong."

The Emperor snatched a tiny piece of dark meat from a serving dish and momentarily held it up to his nose.

"Smells okay to me."

He offered the morsel of chicken to Gwendolyn's cat. The furry animal gulped it down.

The food taster stepped back from the table.

"I pronounce this food safe for consumption—"

The cat screeched and burst into flames.

Chapter Twenty-Six

"Hurry up with that," the old woman said.

Katja flipped aside the hem of her skirts and trotted up the path. Her breath streamed white in the cold air. Every few steps, the frigid water in the bucket she carried sloshed over the rim, dousing the side of her leg. Despite the steep slope along the riverbank, the old woman climbed at a pace that Katja found difficult to match. She was breathing heavily by the time she reached the top.

"Spill too much, and I'll send you back for more," the old woman scolded.

"Sorry," Katja said. "I'll do better."

"Do. It will be good for you."

The Desolation Mountain Range towered high on all sides. Patches of frost sparkled whitely over the ground. A light breeze whispered through the dark green needles of the pine forest.

A narrow path led back to the small lumber town that served as Katja's home for the last weeks. Stout shacks clustered together in a natural clearing furnished living space for the several dozen inhabitants. A giant pile of sawdust stood off to the side of a saw mill. The circular metal blades sat motionless and silent at the moment. A water wheel turned slowly in the stream adjacent to the site.

Never before had Katja been forced to endure such hellish conditions, subjected to a lifestyle so backward that not a single pub existed in the entire area. The steady physical work combined with meals that consisted of raw vegetables picked by her own hand from a garden were hardships so trying as to make even hiding in the crypt back in Empire City seem cozy by comparison. She would soon die from starvation or boredom, she decided, and likely before the week was out. Only the threat of arrest and torture kept her from slipping back into the city. Any city.

The old woman flung open the door of her shack.

"Get busy with splitting that firewood. Don't make me tan your behind with a bramble. Get to it."

Katja placed the bucket on the front step and made her way to the yard in back of the shack. A single glance at the huge mound of wood intended for splitting induced a sigh from her lips. The ancient axe provided for the gruesome chore was as dull as a butter knife and felt heavy as she hefted it over her shoulder.

She placed a piece of firewood on end and swung the axe. The blade bit about an inch into the hard wood and came to an abrupt stop. She pulled back on the handle, but instead of freeing the axe, lifted the log into the air. Cursing, she shook the handle with all her might. The axe head remained stuck fast. Kicking the handle accomplished nothing. She stood on the log and worked the handle back and forth, increasing the pressure in small increments. The axe popped free at last.

Panting, she swung the axe in a second, mighty blow. The iron head once again bit about an inch into the wood. She pulled back on the handle, lifted the log into the air, and nearly screamed in frustration.

"Men on horses coming this way," called the old woman.

Katja dropped the axe and hurried inside the shack. She watched through a crack in a shuttered window as the old woman scurried up to the wood pile. A heartbeat later, a half-dozen imperial guards atop black steeds came riding into the village. A sinking feeling in Katja's stomach grew intense as the soldiers spread out and began knocking on doors, conferring with the occupants of one residence before moving on to the next. The old woman kept up the charade of splitting wood as the horsemen came to a stop a few feet away from where she labored.

"Old woman," a soldier shouted. "We seek a fugitive, a traitor to the crown."

"I didn't do nothing," the old woman shouted back. "I've lived here in Brookhaven all my life, ask anybody. Never heard anything so ridiculous. Traitor indeed."

"I didn't mean you," the man called down. "We seek a fugitive wanted for crimes in Empire City. Harboring criminals is a crime punishable by death. Do you know of or have you seen any newcomers pass through this town?"

"Newcomers always pass through Brookhaven," she said. "It's impossible to keep track of them all, what with the loggers, muleskinners, hawkers, and the like. Now it's you soldiers. Always somebody new coming and going. Been as busy as Empire City around here lately."

"Do you live alone?"

The woman nodded. "Yep, just me and my niece."

The soldier leaned forward in his saddle. "Your niece wouldn't have long, dark hair, would she? Blue eyes? Dresses like a harlot?"

"Are you stupid or something?" The old woman's voice quivered with rage. "How dare you accuse my niece of such behavior. This is a respectable village, as are the women in Brookhaven respectable, and that includes my niece. We are every bit as respectable as the folks in that big city you live in. I've half a mind to pull you off that horse and teach you some respect."

"Never mind." The guard appeared to lose interest. "Carry on with your business."

"Well, thank the gods for small favors." The old woman held up the axe. "In my day, a soldier would get off his horse and help and old woman with her chores, especially with hard work like wood splitting."

"We're soldiers." The soldier wheeled his horse around. "Not lumberjacks. Maybe if we weren't so busy . . . ."

"I pay your salary with my taxes," she shouted. "You work for me. Get back here."

The soldiers rode out of town amid a flourish of clomping hooves, leaving a trail of dust in their wake. Katja was hardly surprised by their quick departure. Brookhaven represented the end of the line not only for herself but for professional soldiers as well, men accustomed to hardship and danger.

The old woman slammed shut the door and dropped the lock bar into place.

"They must really want this fugitive," she said. "To come so far and all."

"Many thanks for not giving me away," Katja said.

The old woman nodded. "I knew you were on the run from something, I just didn't know from who or for what reason. But imperial soldiers? My goodness, you have been a very busy young lady. To be perfectly honest, that first night you showed up, during that big storm, banging on my door and asking for help, I thought it most likely you were on the run from your husband or a boyfriend or something similar."

"That solder," Katja said, "is an ape. He knows nothing of proper dress, nor of fashion. He claims I dress like a harlot? I have attended imperial events dressed in my usual garb, functions where the Emperor himself was present. That soldier has only pranced around in his briefs in front of his boyfriends in the bowels of the local prison."

The old woman smiled. "His description of you means nothing. Let it bother you not."

"No wonder the Empire is on such shaky footing," Katja said. "With men of such low quality defending the realm."

"He was likely kicked in the head by a horse when young," the old woman said. "His words are less than nothing."

Katja nodded. "I thought I was doomed when the soldiers went from house to house. Surely one of your neighbors would have reported the arrival of your new niece? Strangers can't be common around here, despite what you told the guard."

The old woman chuckled. "I mostly told the truth. Prospectors do sometimes come through, hunters and the like, but few others. Which is why I knew that none of my neighbors were going to speak a peep about your arrival. Those soldiers are outsiders, and we in Brookhaven owe them nothing."

"But they threatened death as punishment for harboring a criminal."

The old woman nodded. "That's a big part of the problem with the people running the Empire. The only time they ever notice anyone outside the capital is to demand compliance with some new law, usually a new tax, and back it up with threats. But we are a community here, partly because we can only rely on each other for help, and so betraying our neighbors to win the momentary favor of some government official is not the way things are done."

"You've never been to Empire City," Katja said. "People there are not so honest. Many people are not, at any rate."

"Did you hear the soldier's words regarding the crimes to which you are accused?"

"Treason, among a host of other offenses."

"Did you do these things?"

"Of course not, I'm no traitor. I was set up and wasn't smart enough to see it coming. I took the bait and am a fool for having done so, especially for having struck a deal with a mage in the first place. The Royal Court is a snake pit, a den of degenerates dressed in gold and silver. You can never be sure who to trust, if anyone."

"Yet you willingly made a deal with a magic user? Risky business."

"That was admittedly a big mistake."

"What did this mage offer you in exchange for your cooperation?"

"How do you know it was all his plan?"

The old woman stared.

Katja sighed. "Gold."

"And for what purpose did you need this gold? What is it you desire so much that makes risking your life worthwhile?"

Katja shrugged. "You know, the usual. Nice things. Security against poverty. A life removed from the drudgery of physical toil, free from carrying buckets of water up steep hills and splitting green firewood with a dull axe."

The old woman smiled. "That part of your plan, the avoiding splitting wood and carrying water, hasn't quite worked out. But the exercise is good for you, the walking and the carrying."

"No part of my plan has worked out."

"Not as yet," the old woman said. "But life is long. You don't perspire all the time anymore, like you did when you first came."

Katja nodded. "I think that was the ale working its way out of my system. And there are no pubs around here in which to refuel."

"What will you do now? What are your plans?"

"What options do I really have? So long as you are willing, I should like to stay on as your help, at least until this manhunt nonsense comes to an end. Then I can return to the city without fear of arrest."

"The authorities are rarely so forgiving regarding crimes committed against the state, especially when accusations of treason are involved. You could be here for a long time."

Katja swallowed. "Surely not."

"Perhaps for the rest of your life. You must be prepared for that possibility. The charge of treason, whether true or not, is a crime to which the statute of limitations does not apply. You might be spending the rest of your days in this village."

Katja shook her head. "That . . . cannot be."

"Life in Brookhaven isn't so bad," the old woman soothed. "You'll find a man sooner or later. Frank McCut, he's a tree faller that lives up the road, he's been looking for a new woman for some time now, almost a year. He's got a big brood of kids and nobody to do the cooking and cleaning for them since his wife died. He'd probably take you in. Then there's Crazy Willy, he lives down by the old abandoned mill. Some folks say he's a half-wit old hermit, but others who can understand his speech say that he talks about nothing but getting a woman for himself. He might be interested."

"They're both so tempting." Katja's mind raced. Should she flee tonight? The only path for her now lay eastward, through the mountain passes and to the frontier settlements beyond. And all for what, to visit the fishing village of Bandit? A luxurious life in the blast oven of the Wastelands?

"I tease you," the old woman said. "You can live with me for as long as you like. Though I do not jest when I say those baked pastries you like so much will not prepare themselves. You had better get busy picking us some more blueberries. The bushes atop Steep Point should be ready by now. You had best get busy."

Katja grimaced. "Steep Point?"

"That's right, burn the fat away from your backside climbing the hill, then put it back on with muffins. Pay your debt before leaving the shop, that's what I always say. Take your time. You can split the firewood when you get back."

The path up Steep Point twisted through one switchback after another. Katja's legs quivered with fatigue by the time she reached the top of the slope. She dropped to her knees and regained her breath, assuring herself all the while that the tasty pastries would be worth the effort.

She leaned back on her heels in shock: is this to be my life from here on in, she wondered? Mornings spent fetching water? Days spent picking blueberries? Married to Crazy Larry or whoever else the old woman tried to fix her up with? She shook her head. While the quiet life appealed to some, she had seen too much of the world and experienced too many luxuries to be satisfied with anything but a home in a city.

A tiny puff of smoke far off in the distance caught her attention. Miles to the east, well beyond the last vestiges of civilization, where not a road or trail left a mark, a fire burned. Unlike a forest fire, where entire trees went up in flames and smoke shrouded the countryside, the blaze neither grew nor shrank nor produced big clouds of smoke. A bon fire, she decided. She squinted her eyes but could make out no finer details owing to the extreme distance.

She glanced westward, considering. No path led through those grim peaks. Perhaps a band of hunters, chasing some exotic beast. The possibility seemed remote, especially considering the ease of locating game in more easily accessible areas like Brookhaven.

A crawling sensation ran the length of her spine: if those who started the fire originated from the far side of the Desolation Mountains, they might be anybody. Or anything.

She squinted with renewed determination, trying with all her might to bring the scene into closer focus, but the shimmering heat waves rising from the ground proved impossible to penetrate.

She stamped her foot in frustration. Were they even men at all?

She stared for a long time, the empty bowl held loosely in her hand.

Chapter Twenty-Seven

Parrot worked a writing quill over a parchment. Such was his skill that not a wayward drop of ink or a single smudge befouled the pristine historical document.

Patrons occupied about half the tables in the saloon. A small lamp at each table gave off a flickering orange glow.

"So what happened to the Lady Gwendolyn?" Parrot asked.

Prince Gerald shook his head. "Nothing happened to her. She wasn't burned at all. But the cat went up like a dry stick and ran around in circles, screeching like crazy the entire while. A living torch."

Parrot wrote at a furious pace to keep up, bold strokes all, yet his penmanship suffered not one whit.

"So what's the situation at the castle now that they know they've got a serial murderer on their hands?"

Prince Gerald shrugged. "There was a lot of confusion, and accusations and counter-accusations being made. The Emperor ordered an immediate investigation. I came back here."

"We hardly ate anything before it happened," complained Thundar, scowling from his perch atop the prince's shoulder. "I'd have eaten better tonight hunting the skies myself. Catch a cat or something."

"My arm and shoulder are numb from the weight of you," Gerald said. "Get off me and go sit on a bench or something."

The dragon dropped to the floor with a crash and waddled over to a stool. Wings spread, he jumped into the air, exerting mightily judging by the expression of strain on his face, but managed to ascend only half the way to the top of the stool before falling back to the floor.

"Whoops," Thundar said. "The draft coming under the door threw me off. Here we go for real."

A blast of wind pushed back Parrot's hair as Thundar launched into flight. The dragon made it nearly to the top of the stool before losing altitude. Dragon claws scrabbled against the edge of the smooth seat, but before Thundar managed to gain purchase, he flipped upside down and crashed headfirst to the floor.

"That's really sad," Prince Gerald said. "You can't even fly anymore?"

"I slipped." Thundar rubbed his head. "Well, the first time I lost my balance. This time I slipped."

"Slipped while you were flying?"

"No, when I tried to take off." The dragon extended a claw in the direction of the floor. "Right there, somebody must have spilled grease there or something. Anyhow, too much dust was flying around last time to even see properly so . . . ."

Thundar proceeded to physically climb up the stool, pulling his portly body aloft through the use of his long claws. Once safely atop the seat, he fell to his back, breathing heavily.

"You really need to go on a diet," Prince Gerald observed.

The front door of the saloon swung open. Rogan, Skunk, and Red wandered inside. Prince Gerald addressed the warriors in a friendly tone.

"You men missed an interesting banquet."

Rogan's eyebrows pulled low over his protruding brown ridge. "Rumors are flying regarding some sort of incident at the castle. The say a group of terrorists are poisoning off royalty?"

"Who says?"

"Some guy we talked to in a different pub a little while ago," Rogan said. "Somebody tried to poison the Emperor again? Is that true?"

"I don't think the Emperor was the target," Gerald said.

"You'd have had to see it to believe it," Thundar added.

"What's got to him?" Rogan indicated the prostate dragon. "Had a tough day?"

"You could say it's another one of those things you'd have had to see to believe," Gerald said.

"It's all recorded in the chronicles," Parrot said.

"Accurately, I hope?"

Rogan's lame attempt at humor hung awkwardly in the air.

"I know of no other way."

"The situation here is a little more unsettled than we knew," Gerald said. "I'm thinking it's time we pulled out and headed back to Bogwood. This entire mess seems bound to get worse before it gets better, and there's no sense in our getting caught up in it."

"We haven't been here all that long," Rogan said. "It's too bad that we must leave so soon."

Red and Skunk jointly announced their intention to visit the jakes. The pair exited the inn through a side door. A server arrived at the table with a pitcher of ale and four empty mugs. Rogan doled out a coin for the drinks, cursing the entire while.

"Disappear to the jakes when it's time to pay, even I haven't used that one yet."

"Don't let the cost get to you," Thundar said. "You can always find another monster to slay and collect the reward."

"Easier said than done," Rogan jabbered. "I had my hands full with that swamp pincher. Speaking of earning one's keep, what happened to your reconnaissance duties? You haven't been doing any flying at all lately, not from what I've seen."

"Inside this building? Are you mad? I could hit a door frame or a lamp. I might break a wing or worse."

"I meant fly around the city."

"For what purpose? It's not like I can go ahead and scout out our path like on our journey here. No, the prince is keeping me fresh for the return trip to North Bogsonia, tanned, rested, and ready."

A hollering broke out behind the pub, a chorus of muffled shouts delivered in a tone of panic. Feet tromped past the front door. More yelling.

Rogan sprang to his feet, axe in hand.

"Red and Skunk are out there. They'd better not be causing any trouble."

Parrot followed Gerald and Rogan as the pair charged out the door.

A group of men holding lit torches clustered in front of a pair of clapboard outhouses, shaking their heads and muttering darkly. The outhouse doors were propped open. Gerald and Rogan pushed their way to the front of the small crowd but moved no farther. Parrot craned his neck to see past the people blocking his way.

Red and Skunk were dead, decapitated as they sat on the toilet, identifiable in their distinctive tan brown tunics. The heads of the murdered men were nowhere in sight.

Blood glistened wetly on the interior walls and splattered the ceilings. Parrot wondered briefly over the motive for an attack of such extreme violence. Robbery would have availed the killers no more than a few coppers. As newcomers to the city, Red and Skunk had yet to quarrel with anyone. Neither men were known to have kin in the city. A blood feud seemed impossible.

The pounding of horse's hooves preceded the arrival of a troupe of soldiers.

The leader of the column trotted his mount directly up to the jakes. He looked from side to side. "Prince Gerald, there you are. Councilor Jones sends his greetings, along with his thanks for saving his life. It is a relief to find you unharmed, but I see we are too late. Those were your men in there?"

"Who did this?" Gerald said. "If Councilor Jones knew my men were in peril, why didn't he mention it earlier?"

The soldier pursed his lips. "I do not know the identity of the murderers, but that your men are the victims of a professional killing seems obvious enough." He pointed. "Their weapons are still sheathed, so it appears they were killed simultaneously after being taken by surprise. Unlikely that one of your men would have stayed seated while the other was being slain. As for the decapitations, assassins sometimes keep the head of their victims as proof of their deeds for their employer."

"Why Red?" Rogan said. "Why Skunk? They were just regular soldiers."

The soldier shrugged. "You'd need to ask the assassins for a definite answer, but I strongly suspect that these men were not the original target. It stands to reason that you, Prince Gerald, would likely be first on their list. Mistaken identity perhaps, or maybe your entire group was to be taken out."

"We should think about getting back home," Thundar said.

The guard shook his head. "That's not what you want to do, not right now. Not if your plans include staying alive. Somebody wants you dead. Professional assassins don't work cheap. Something lethal would almost certainly befall your party before you made it very far, perhaps an ambush just outside the city limits or on the trail shortly thereafter."

"What else?" Rogan said. "Stay here and wait for more assassins to come and finish the job?"

The guard turned to Prince Gerald.

"Councilor Jones invites you and your men to lodge at his villa as his guests for the remainder of your stay in Empire City. I only regret that there are two less of your men to escort than there might be had we acted earlier. Within a week or two, during some night when the city is asleep, Councilor Jones will arrange for you to leave under the cover of darkness. Stay here, and you'll end up like these others."

"We'll take it," Thundar said.

Chapter Twenty-Eight

Zirac stared down on Empire City.

Twinkling torches set in lampposts beat back the night from the city streets, illuminating the pathways for the pathetic wretches that infested the capital, for those clueless clods that did not yet realize their destiny lay in serving their betters. But they would soon learn.

With the troublesome prince from Bogsonia—twice now a thorn in his side—out of the way for good, the path was clear to remove Councilor Jones and substitute his own man on the council without any meddling from outsiders.

He glanced over at the shelf, admiring the misshapen thing in the jar on one level of his mind while on another level saddened that the Bogsonian would not be inhabiting a jar of his own. It was the only appropriate fate for one foolish enough to seek to thwart the will of a supermage.

He burst into laughter.

Were he to gather together in one place all of the people in the Empire willing to betray their supposed principles for some slight monetary gain, or simply because the opportunity presented itself, the lineup would extend twice around the planet. From the average housewife shamming shock over her neighbor's marital infidelity to the working man's typical denouncements of murder and other capital crimes, it was his experience that people were as steadfast in their convictions as a wet piece of clay. They opposed only those behaviors which they had not yet had the opportunity to practice themselves. And they had the gall to criticize him? He shook his head, scarcely able to stomach the hypocrisy. At least he was honest in that everyone knew on some level what he was all about. He did not go around dressed like a respectable merchant while robbing the citizens blind. That people were doormats in his world, and their rightful place only but to serve his whims, were as straightforward as any other part of his demeanor. No need for weasel words.

The waif floated into the room.

"A man wishes an audience."

"Send him in."

The assassin veritably glided into the room, his every movement nearly as light and fluid as that of the waif. A massive scar covered one side of the man's face, lending his appearance an especially sinister countenance. There could be no mistaking the dangerous gleam in those flat eyes, the calculating gaze of a professional killer. A bulging burlap sack slung over one shoulder dribbled a crimson liquid on the floor.

"Child's play." The assassin held out the sack. "Pay me."

"Let me see." Zirac struggled to control his excitement. An idea passed through his mind, a thought so stupendous and brilliant that only the gods knew why he had failed to conceive of it earlier: the Bogsonian's head could be preserved in a jar of pure alcohol, and thereby capturing forever the expression of fear and surprise that invariably accompanied sudden and unexpected death. It was a worthy trophy, even if not as spectacular a keepsake as a lump of living flesh in a jar.

The assassin dumped the contents of the sack on the floor. Zirac bent down and examined one head, then the other, and examined both heads again.

"You are a fool."

The assassin stared.

"Neither of these men is Prince Gerald," Zirac said. "You idiot. You have succeeded only in warning them. These two are nothing."

"I carried out my instructions," the assassin said. "My brother and I were told to take out a foreigner or foreigners in brown tunics, and that we did. Pay me."

Zirac shook his head. "You were told to take the head of the swamp monkey from North Bogsonia, not that of his underlings. You can't tell the difference between a prince and these two?"

The assassin shrugged. "They were all dressed the same. You said that neither the wielder of the axe nor their chronicler were the targets. They were not taken."

"You didn't get the job done," Zirac hollered. "Understand? All you did was warn the swamp monkey that there's a price out on his head."

"There's no guarantee of success with the guild," the assassin said. "You know that. Pay up."

Zirac snorted. "You should be paying me for all the damage you did. I still need to find somebody willing to make the hit that you missed, but now because of your stupidity, it will be immeasurably harder to get close to the target."

"Pay me what you owe."

"I owe you nothing. Get out."

"Last chance. Pay me. Right now." The assassin moved under his robes.

"Get out," Zirac repeated. "Amateur."

The assassin's arm moved in a blur, slashing a long knife in an arc aimed squarely at Zirac's unprotected neck. Zirac didn't even bother trying to defend himself.

Before the blade traveled even half the distance to its intended fleshly target, the waif was on the assassin, not beating him or smothering him, not overpowering the man with physical strength, but simply being with him, rolling over him like a monstrous ether. The effect was as immediate as it was drastic.

The assassin screamed long and loud, a howl of agony and fear and wild regret rolled into one. His voice cut off as his entire body solidified, mouth open, lips pulled back, in an instant stuck tight as if cast in concrete. Frozen solid.

The waif drifted silently away. The corpse toppled to the floor and shattered in a thousand tiny pieces. Zirac shook his head, disgusted. Who was going to clean up this mess? The waif literally couldn't even hold a broom. Something was wrong when the most powerful sorcerer in the land was stuck with the chore of sweeping up the pieces of a defeated enemy. The Emperor's cleaning staff refused to enter his tower. He was told they would rather quit their employ at the castle than enter his "lair." He could hardly fathom the audacity. The very idea that an inferior person might choose to disregard orders from their betters without suffering fatal consequences as a result would be among the first misconceptions he would clarify upon taking the throne.

But now what?

The assassin's guild would likely blame him for what had happened, perhaps even claim he murdered one of their members, despite the fact that it was their own thug who attacked first. Despite the truth. Such is the price of associating with lowlifes, he consoled himself.

That the corpse had already been reduced to small chunks of flesh was a definite benefit, facilitating a quick cleanup. A handful of assassin bits in the hearth here, a few more there, and in short order, nothing would be left but a small mound of ashes.

Zirac stopped short. What about the assassin's partner? Two assassins were involved in the botched hit. The second man undoubtedly waited somewhere nearby, forevermore to anticipate the return of his brother . . .

Caution dictated that the second man should be liquidated as well, but how to pin it all on someone else? He might have thought to ask the first assassin the location of his partner before killing the man, he supposed. Were the guild to declare war over the disappearance of their members, the fools would set off a messy and altogether unproductive struggle, one which could delay the implementation of his plans that much longer. His own life was in no danger, but what gain in a protracted battle?

Best to claim ignorance. What responsibility were it of his that the assassin had been waylaid and murdered, killed for the loot he foolishly flashed around in a pub or brothel? Or perhaps the man had fled town, skipped out with the loot in his pocket, choosing to steal the money rather than turn it over to the guild. Zirac was as blameless in the entire affair as a young princess, and the waif was his witness. He laughed.

That the Lady Gwendolyn would be his property sooner or later was a given, but how best to manipulate events so as to facilitate that end sooner rather than later? Despite his own genius-level intelligence, cultured tastes, and debonair appearance, the woman acted as though she despised his very company. Her shameful behavior in front of the—still alive!—swamp monkey grated like a stone in his shoe. The sight of the woman twirling her fingers in her hair as she stared in the Bogsonian's direction, her suddenly outthrust chest each time he happened to glance her way, her entire attitude was nearly enough to make a grown man sick. And to top it off, the yokel remained oblivious of her attentions, more interested in conversing with the bloated serpent on his shoulder and eating food than in associating with the most desirable woman in the entire Empire. Why were people so stupid?

The waif floated back into the room.

"A man is here to see you."

"What man?"

"A man."

Zirac felt a twinge of irritation at his own question. The waif was incapable of communicating more than the most basic information. He assumed the second assassin had come calling and considered how best to dispose of the corpse, but remembered that he had indeed slotted a second appointment for the evening.

"Show him in."

Don't kill this one, Zirac lectured himself. Take your rightful vengeance on these fools later. Show restraint until the right time arrives. They are needed—for now.

The visitor made a wide detour around the bits o' assassin spread out on the floor. He came to a stop several paces back from the desk.

"You sent for me?"

"The time is now," Zirac said. "Release the beast while the Emperor's picnic is in full swing. Are you quite certain it has been adequately trained to recognize Councilor Jones from the other guests?"

The man smiled, exposing large gaps between blackened teeth.

"The robe and tunic you provided have been thrown into its pen at feeding time for the last two weeks. The beast now solidly connects the scent of the councilor with that of food. Sharpest sense of smell in the animal kingdom, or so they say. It's salivating like a waterfall just as soon as the councilor's musk reaches its nose."

"Who is to say that it will not turn on the others at the party, on myself specifically, after it has succeeded in killing the councilor?"

"It'll only be interested in feeding after it makes a kill. It'll gorge itself on the councilor until someone comes along and pincushions it with arrows."

"So long as you are certain. Once it's distracted, I'll be free to rescue the fair princess. How could she not be grateful for such a heroic deed?"

"You are truly a gent."

"Afterward, I will demand her hand in marriage. How could the Emperor refuse after I have saved both of their lives?"

"Remember your friends when you attain the throne, Zirac."

"The throne? Why, the thought hadn't even crossed mind. But rest assured, I always remember my friends. Trust me."

Chapter Twenty-Nine

Katja slid over the edge of rocky outcrop and plunged into empty space. A grunt escaped her lips as she landed after a six foot drop.

The forest rustled in the breeze. Openings in the tree canopy allowed scattered patches of sunlight to reach the ground. Ferns, rose bushes, and stalks of millet taller than a person competed with alder bushes and willow. Narrow animal trails created intersecting paths between the trees and shrubs. Chirping birds and buzzing flies and hordes of insanity-provoking mosquitoes made their presence know through a nonstop barrage of activity.

A misshapen pine tree she had used as a landmark stood atop a nearby knoll, the trunk split down the middle by a lightning strike or some other calamity in its youth so that two fully mature but intricately intertwined trunks grew from a single stump. There was no confusing that she was indeed in the intended area. So where was the fire she spotted from afar?

The old woman had made clear her displeasure over Katja's decision to leave Brookhaven, and for her decision to plunge into the wilds in order to investigate what was in all likelihood nothing more than a mere campfire, and most severely for her refusal to get down to what the old woman considered a proper life for a woman, that being marriage to Frank McCut or Crazy Willy or whoever else might need a cook, babysitter, seamstress, and nurse all rolled into one. Katja laughed aloud. She would never marry McCut or any other man for the sake of convenience. She would marry for money.

She stalked slowly between the trees. Her soft boots made no noise on the thick carpet of pine needles. A pair of aspen leaning together creaked in the wind, but otherwise all was quiet.

The sour reek of decay caused her to stop in her tracks.

The stench was unmistakable. Why would an active hunting party keep rotten meat in their camp? Deer, elk, and moose roamed the forest in abundance. Rabbits aplenty hid among the spiny protection offered by scimitar thickets, easy pickings for any halfway competent human hunter. An average twelve-year-old with a slingshot would keep a full belly under such circumstances. Something definitely wasn't adding up.

She crouched low to the ground and crept around a stand of willows. The lightning-split pine stood ten paces to her left. She squinted her eyes, searching for any sign of movement. Nothing. She moved behind a jumble of trees. Still no sign of a guard or sentry. The smell of decay mixed with woodsmoke hit her senses again, stronger than ever. She spotted a clearing in the forest and moved as quietly as possible up to the edge of the trees.

The sight within the clearing caused her to gag.

Some exceedingly unfortunate individual had been cooked on a spit over an open fire and partially consumed. Unquestionably human, the body was impaled lengthways on a rough-hewn pole and laid horizontally over still-smoldering coals. One leg was missing. A human femur bone lay the dirt nearby. Split lengthwise, the marrow within had been removed. The remnants of flesh still attached to the corpse had a torn look, as if skin and muscles were ripped away in a frenzy of feeding. Flies swarmed through the air.

Other than the corpse and the flies, the clearing was deserted. She crept up to the fire and noticed additional signs of human remains, a skull, gnawed finger bones, a rib. The murder victim on the spit was not the first to die here. Who would do such a thing?

She spotted a broken arrow on the ground. The arrowhead was missing and two of the three stabilizer feathers were gone, but the lone black raven feather attached to the black shaft of eastern tamarack was as distinctive as it was deadly. Only one race used such arrows.

She turned and raced back into the forest.

Chapter Thirty

"Yes, of course I'll have another," Thundar said.

The servant turned to Gerald.

"More ale for yourself as well, sir?"

Gerald answered with a shake of his head. "I greatly appreciate your hospitality this week, councilor."

"Not at all." Councilor Jones slurped from a wide crystal chalice seated atop a couch on the opposite side of the room. "Small compensation compared to the favor you did me. I've been thinking about how to repay that debt. What is adequate recompense for saving a man's life? Any gift, no matter how grand, would be trivial by comparison. It seems that I am bound to remain indebted to you."

"Call it even." Gerald let loose a long belch. "You saved our lives getting us out of that inn. Besides, there is no such thing as permanent indebtedness where I come from."

"The people of North Bogsonia are so magnanimous?"

"No, they just have short memories." Gerald laughed. "But seriously, they are good folks, the vast majority of them at any rate."

"As it is in Empire City," Councilor Jones said. "But the few mischief makers certainly do stir the pot, don't they? So what is an average day like in North Bogsonia? Do you find it unnerving being geographically situated alongside the ogres, goblins, and trolls?"

Gerald shrugged. "The trolls are only a nuisance until some troublemaking goblin starts training them for an army, which hasn't happened for some centuries now. Ogres sicken and die when they enter North Bogsonia, and goblins fare little better. The enemies of mankind will rise up and attack the Empire again one day, but we in Bogwood will be safe behind our walls. We will sit back and allow the lushness of the land to sap the strength and lives of the attackers until they are forced to give up and go home."

Councilor Jones nodded. "The establishment of North Bogsonia and South Bogsonia were the true masterstrokes of King Dexter's reign, along with the founding of Wizardhome." He lounged back on his couch. "Despite it all, I'm surprised anyone managed to survive in those parts you call home in the first place. No offense intended, but it is said the rigors of living in a wild swamp is the reason for the hardiness of your people."

Gerald laughed aloud. "My friend, you heard false rumors, hateful propaganda. North Bogsonia is admittedly a harsh taskmaster for the ignorant and the weak, but could the same not be said of Empire City? For the right kind of person, my homeland is an oasis of life, rife with game, countless in number and species. Everywhere else I have been is like a wasteland in comparison."

"It must get somewhat muggy there in the summertime?"

"Not at all. The air carries only a pleasant moisture. The steam that rises up from the swamp on hot days is a joy to experience."

"Sounds really muggy."

"It is," Thundar said. "I flew over that way once. It's a swamp alright."

Gerald smiled. "All just a matter of perspective. Were I a native of the Blasted Lands, or from the province of Plenty, a misnamed patch of sun-roasted dirt if there ever was such a thing, then I'd likely consider the arid conditions hereabouts to be normal. But as a citizen of North Bogsonia, my outlook is somewhat more worldly. You need not take my word for it, come for a visit to our fair land. You'd be a welcome guest, councilor."

"Oh." Councilor Jones looked pained. "That's tempting and all, but business responsibilities keep me here. In perpetuity."

"A shame," Gerald said. "There's no chance that you might be able to get away for even a little while and come and see us?"

"No chance, no. But on another subject, where do you presently fit in regards to the succession of the throne of North Bogsonia?"

"Third born."

Councilor Jones whistled. "Better get busy then, chop, chop, if you get my drift."

"I don't get your drift at all."

"Fratricide is a common means of advancing one's birthright among the royal families in Empire City. The issue is often settled long before the participants mature to adulthood, with sibling killing sibling until only one remains alive. Your life is in no immediate danger from your brothers?"

Gerald frowned. "Not so far as I know. I'm too far down the line of succession to even matter. My older brothers might stare at each other with some suspicion, and perhaps they both crave the throne, but our lineage is a long lived one, and my father will cling to power until his death, and well after his children have grown to an advanced age. As his father did before him."

"A wise enough solution, so long as the king does not find himself the object of a coup by his children."

Gerald smiled. "Perhaps the royals in Empire City have more to fight over than we do in North Bogsonia, some greater grievances against one another and such. Or maybe it's that that we don't allow magicians to mix among us, or permit them to spin their foul webs of treachery at royal functions."

Councilor Jones waved his hand dismissively. "Even before Zirac came along, the shenanigans of the royal families, specifically their efforts to influence the will of the Emperor, had already reached an intolerable level. Murder, assassination, the grim reality is that many royals simply disappear, never to be heard from again. Corpses garbed in rich dress are occasionally discovered floating in sewers and the like, but invariably are so physically damaged that a positive identification is impossible."

"How do the killings advance their position?" Gerald asked. "Murder holds sway with the Emperor?"

The councilor shrugged. "A dead rival holds no influence. Murdering one's enemies is the most efficient way to silence antagonistic opinions. It's all about power, the situation exacerbated by the Emperor's increasingly fragile health and the urgent need for the Lady Gwendolyn to take a husband and produce an heir. But no faction will support a candidate from another family for her hand. So what to do?"

"Pity the fool who agrees to take on the roll of Lady Gwendolyn's suitor." Gerald chuckled. "He would be the target of assassination from the moment his name was announced to the public."

"The best solution," the councilor said, "would be for the princess to wed a man with no formal ties to any of the royal factions, a noble with no preference for one house over another. None of them will be wholly satisfied without one of their own destined for the throne, but they must be realistic and understand that civil war might result if one family were to gain an advantage. The situation is very delicate. Some factions might even rally around this outsider, both in a show of patriotism and in relief that their sworn enemies are not destined to become the next Imperial Family."

"Good luck finding such a person," Gerald said. "He would need to have a death wish."

Councilor Jones sat up on his couch. "A man with vision and courage might make a play for the throne. Such a chance surely can arise only once in any man's lifetime. With a little luck, a certain young prince might gain the most powerful position in the world."

"This visionary you speak of would end up dead in short order," Gerald said. "For every person who succeeds in winning a throne, ten more die in the attempt to win one, and often badly at that, crucified or skinned alive or some such. And all for what? To gain a target on their backside? To have poison placed in their food?"

"A person hardly needs to wed the princess to see their food poisoned, as I know only too well."

"Granted, but you know what I say is true. A brave man might make a play for the throne, but a wise man would dismiss the concept entirely and return home. Speaking of which, what is your counsel regarding my return to North Bogsonia? The Emperor's birthday is past, and I itch to be on my way. My journey to Bogwood is a long one."

"Soon, right after the Royal Picnic. Attendance by all royals is expected."

"The what?"

"The Royal Picnic is yet another function sponsored by the castle. It's an annual event, but at least it's the last one of the season. You might be best off telling people there that you've decided to stick around Empire City for a couple of more weeks, and then we'll slip you out of the city the same night."

"I need to attend this picnic?" Gerald asked.

Councilor Jones looked pained. "I'm afraid so. You are royalty, and so not going would be viewed as an insult to the Emperor. You don't want to do that."

Gerald smiled. "I sure don't. When's this picnic?"

"The afternoon after tomorrow. You might bring your men along with you this time. As a representative of a head of state, you really should avoid attending royal events stag."

"I tried to speak to him about this already," Thundar said. "It did no good."

"Do I bring food to this picnic?" Gerald said.

The councilor chuckled. "It's a picnic, not a potluck. The event raises money for some of the city's more trusted charities. Royals attend and donate to various causes. The bigger the donation, the better."

"It sounds like we should leave before the picnic," Thundar said. "Save ourselves some loot."

"No need," Councilor Jones said. "I'll make a donation in all our names, a large one. Once again, it's the least I can do after you saved my life. But your presence at the picnic is expected, and there's nothing I can do about that."

Gerald led his small entourage to an empty table and took a seat.

The Royal Picnic took place among the manicured trees and cut grass lawns of the Emperor's personal hunting preserve, located barely a stone's throw from the easternmost wall of the castle. Servants set up rows of tables and chairs on the sand along a gently gurgling brook. The water ran so clear as to be virtually invisible. Small fish flitted in the current. Birdsong called for attention from all directions.

"Wild country," Rogan commented.

"Land to test a man," Parrot agreed. "Harsh."

"Look at all the empty chairs," Thundar complained. "I hate it when we're the first to arrive and have to wait forever to get fed. I hope we actually get to eat this time."

"You weren't even really invited," Gerald said. "You don't have to be here at all, remember?"

Thundar shook his head. "The councilor said you ought to bring your people. So here I am."

"No, the councilor mentioned to bring my men. Red dragons are not men, not so far as I know."

"He was only speaking in generalities." Thundar shuffled his feet atop his chair. "He'd have specifically included me if he thought you'd get hung up on a technicality. I'm a big part of your posse. Besides, you saw the way the princess looked at me. She wants me to be here."

Rogan laughed. "She'll take you for a pet and keep you in a cage if you don't behave yourself."

"You look different without your chain mail," Thundar said. "You sound the same, but look different."

"It's my axe that I feel naked without." Rogan slapped the back of his tunic as if searching for the weapon. "Don't take your axe to the picnic, my liege insists, try to look civilized for a change. But that guy standing over there is armed." He pointed.

"He's on duty," Gerald said. "He's a guard. You're here as a guest. Don't worry about it. What could possibly happen at a picnic so that you'll need your axe?"

"Bad precedent is all," Rogan grumbled.

Parrot waved his arm. "This event carries some special importance for my career as a chronicler. My account of what happens here today will be among the most widely studied parts of my work back home, for you can bet that once news of this event circulates among the nobles in Bogwood, similar picnics will become vogue there as well."

"At least someone is impressed," Rogan said. "Can't say as I ever expected to be invited to a picnic."

"Me neither." Thundar tipped back his helmet.

"You weren't invited," Rogan said.

"Let's not get on that again." Gerald glanced over the tables. "Councilor Jones was supposed to meet us here, but it doesn't look like he's made it yet."

"One of us should go sit in that big golden chair at the end of that table." Thundar pointed. "He'd see you sitting there."

Gerald smiled. "Taking the Emperor's throne would get the councilor's attention alright, along with that of everybody else, including the guards."

A steady trickle of guests made their way down the path to the picnic area. Despite the outdoor venue, the newcomers arrived as if prepared for a formal ball, dressed in shimmering cloth cut in the newest styles and laden with jewels and the usual precious metals.

Gerald tugged at his plain tunic. "I feel a little underdressed."

"I know what you mean," Thundar said.

"No, you're good," Rogan said. "We're all good. This is supposed to be a picnic. These city slickers are just ignorant. They don't know style from a hole in the ground."

Still more guests arrived. Servants raced to and fro among the tables, delivering an assortment of refreshments. Jugglers and acrobats performed wondrous feats, dancing, spinning, tumbling, and cartwheeling. Daredevils juggled axes and gleaming blades to the applause of children and adult alike. Parrot scrawled without pause on a parchment. Thundar looked mesmerized by all the activity. The little dragon's mouth hung open.

A group of musicians toting oversized brass horns marched up to the head table and let loose a discordant blast of noise. The guests rose to their feet. As the last notes of music faded away, the Emperor made his appearance, moving slowly in the direction of the throne, at all times surrounded by a crowd of assistants. The Lady Gwendolyn followed, a frown marring her features. A few paces to her rear shuffled the dark form of Zirac.

"The rumors are true. The Emperor looks near death," Thundar said. "Even worse than before."

The guests reseated themselves.

"Dragons aren't known for their subtlety, are they?" Gerald said.

"Dragons are as subtle as they want to be," Thundar said. "We simply choose to be direct. What's the point in claiming the Emperor looks like a strapping young drake when we all know he looks more like a corpse?" He turned his head. "There's the councilor now."

Gerald called out and waved. Councilor Jones smiled as he took a seat at Thundar's side.

"Prince Gerald, gentlemen, I hope you're all having a pleasant day."

"You're late," Thundar said. "What happened?"

"I was taking care of some business back home. Items have been disappearing from my villa. I'm trying to determine whether my mind is playing tricks on me, or if I have a thief among my servants. My staff has been with me for so long that I truly hope it's the former."

"It's probably your mind playing tricks," Thundar said. "If not, that's worse. A thief among your staff, why, he'd likely be robbing you blind right now, taking your stuff at this very moment, looting your possessions even as we sit here talking."

"That's a disturbing possibility," the councilor said. "Except that everything missing to date has been of no value. Old items of clothing, a tattered robe, some blankets I used one night. It's not the monetary loss but the theft itself that concerns me."

"I'd be worried," Thundar said. "Very worried."

"Have some wine," Gerald said. "Wash the concerns from your throat. That's what my father does, and he's a king."

"Yes, of course." Councilor Jones smiled weakly. "I hate to say it, but the Emperor is looking just dreadful today."

"That's not very subtle," Thundar said.

"Pardon me?"

Gerald glanced over at the throne. The Emperor sat slouched over, his crowned head lolling from side to side as if drunk or incapacitated by sickness or extreme old age. Princess Gwendolyn directed the servants tending to her father. Her dress and the silver tiara atop her head sparkled whenever she moved. Zirac occupied a chair at her far side, unspeaking, and by all appearances, ignored.

"She is a beautiful woman," Thundar said.

"Who? Gwendolyn?" Gerald laughed. "She is death for any man foolish enough to get close to her."

Rogan chuckled. "She's almost desirable enough to make it worthwhile."

"Nobody's that desirable," Gerald said. "Not even close. Exchange the rest of your life for a few days as some pampered woman's special pet, all the while waiting for assassins to strike you down? Not likely."

"Not when you put it that way, no," Rogan said. "It seems that all women are trouble when you really give the matter some serious thought."

"Here comes the servants," Thundar said. "About time. I'm about to waste away to nothing."

"You just keep on baiting me, don't you?" Rogan said.

Thundar looked surprised. "What are you talking about?"

"You know."

"What's that over there?" Gerald pointed eastward.

Rogan turned. "What? Where?"

"There. On the horizon. Is that a dragon flying this way?"

Chapter Thirty-One

Katja crept around a jumble of sandstone boulders.

A burst of guttural speech broke out somewhere just ahead. She crouched low to the ground, listening, but found she was unable to comprehend a single word of the pig-like grunts, snorts, and squeals.

A stand of thistle and scraggly jimsonweed growing in the shelter of an oversized rock overhang offered the only hope for quick cover. She scurried like a crab, torn between the desperate need for haste and an equal desire to maintain a low profile.

A rock turned underfoot. She stumbled and hopped among the jimsonweed—and landed upon an oddly soft surface, springy but firm, her initial surprise replaced by dread at the sight of the crudely stitched leggings sticking out from under her feet.

The ogre came awake in an instant, roaring like a lion. Green of skin, seven feet tall, and massive across the chest and shoulders, it grabbed her hair in its huge hands.

Katja ripped free the dagger from her belt and swung the weapon in a looping chop. The blade left a thin red line across the ogre's arm but failed to penetrate deeply. The ogre slapped her hand, knocking the dagger flying. Grasping her hair, the ogre lifted her straight into the air.

Katja kicked her legs and pulled down on the creature's hand, but the vice-like grip only increased in tension. She concentrated on forcing back a single one of the ogre's fingers, twisting and pulling on the digit in an effort to break the bone, but so ineffective were her actions that she might as well have been struggling with an iron rod.

Additional ogres arrived on the scene, grunting and squealing. Katja was held up as if for inspection and shaken like a rag doll, and it was all she could do to maintain her grip on the beast's hand to keep her scalp from tearing away from her head. One ogre among the newcomers leaned close to her face and slobbered a stream of piglike gibberish, the meaning of which was completely lost on her.

Her ogre captor tossed her over its shoulder, and they set off among the sandstone boulders, moving deeper among the bluffs and crags. They crossed over a hill. The aroma of wood smoke grew strong. She was dumped on the ground. As she landed, her head bounced off the rocky surface. Her vision grew dim. Somebody or something kicked her legs, the force of the assault spinning her around. She shielded her face with an arm, but no more blows fell. She passed out.

Someone was shaking her arm. She opened her eyes a crack. A glimpse of the sun hovering over the horizon confirmed her suspicions: hours had passed since her capture during the early part of the afternoon.

"Are you okay?"

A hazy form came into focus, a young woman, a mountain girl judging from her tunic, the garment cut in the same shapeless style favored by all the women in Brookhaven and the surrounding villages.

"Did they hurt you?" The woman said.

"Just where I hit my head." Katja rubbed the lump above her right ear. "Who are you?"

"I am Shep, wife of Chop, the butcher of Newbounty Village."

Katja shook her head in an attempt to clear her mind. Spikes of pain flashed through her brain, followed by a wave of dizziness and nausea. She squeezed shut her eyelids until the spell passed. She looked around once again, careful to keep her head completely still.

She was a prisoner in a war camp, that much was obvious at a glance. Ogres were everywhere, sharpening weapons, polishing armor, eating rations, standing on guard, and hauling firewood, in short, engaged in the usual tasks of an advance army. The small party she mistook for a group of human hunters were only a splinter group, a scouting party or a hunting expedition of a much larger ogre host.

"How did they get through the pass?" Katja said. "How did they get around Bandit?"

"Traitors," the woman declared. "How else?"

Katja nodded. "I have a pretty good idea of the identity of one of those traitors. Not that there's anything I can do about it right now, but I see Zirac's hand in all this. I wonder what they plan to do with us?"

The woman's face went slack. "They'll eat us, just like they ate the others. They'll eat us next."

"There were others? How many?"

"We were captured six nights ago, me and some other women from the village. We were picking berries, and did not see them until it was too late. They brought us here. They have eaten one of us each day since. I am the last one left. They will eat me tonight, or you, but in any case, their choice will only delay the inevitable."

Ignoring the pain in her head, Katja sat up and glanced around the camp with a renewed sense of urgency. Crude tents made from raw animal skins formed shelters for barracks. No trees in sight. No hills. Her preferred plan of action when caught in a pinch—running away—appeared impossible at the moment. The bare rocks and crags offered not a single item of cover. And while ogres did not physically stand directly over her, several of the beasts glanced in her direction at any given moment. Escape under such intense scrutiny seemed out of the question.

A column of ogres came marching into camp, resulting in flurry of activity. The camp ogres raced around, straightening tents, picking up trash, and tidying up in general. Katja had never heard of ogres inclined toward cleanliness or appearances, and only then did she notice a few other oddities that escaped her attention earlier. The camp was relatively clean, even by human standards, and miraculously so for ogres, the messiest of all creatures. The bones from their meals, the viscera from their prey, even the ogres' own feces had been removed from the immediate area, a dedication to sanitation unheard of for the race, and a startling contrast to the filth and rot in the smaller camp she came across earlier.

The camp ogres lined up and lifted their right arms in a sort of honorary salute, palms held flat. The new arrivals strode into camp and came to a stop. Katja stared in disbelief. That anyone would have the ability to teach a pack of ogres the concept of traditional military discipline seemed ridiculous.

An ogre in full battle dress standing head and shoulders taller than those around him led the new arrivals. His massive, barrel-shaped body was encased in plate armor. A horned helm rested atop his head. The camp ogres bowed as if in worship. One among them grunted and squealed and extended an arm in the direction of Katja and the mountain woman.

The giant ogre crossed the camp in a dozen long strides and came to a stop in front of Katja. The camp ogres slavered on the giant's heels, squealing and snorting as if in an atrocious parody of a pig farm. Katja struggled to her feet, certain she was about to be chosen as the main course for the evening meal. Only a single weapon remained available to her still, a wafer-thin stiletto stashed in a secret compartment on the underside of her belt. The world spun. She took a step back in order to regain her balance, tripped over the cowering mountain woman, and fell with a crash.

The giant ogre grasped Katja's hair and yanked her upright with such force that her toes barely touched the ground. She raked her fingers over the massive hand. The ogre's skin might as well have been made of raw oak.

The ogre let loose a particularly loud bark and lowered Katja to the ground. She rubbed her hand over her throbbing head and looked up at the beast. It neither moved away nor touched her as it addressed the monstrous horde, squealing and grunting, the longest verbal communication she had witnessed among the swine to date.

The giant's appearance was unusual for an ogre, its facial features flatter than those of its brethren, the nose smaller, the brow ridge less pronounced, the legs longer and less bowed. The skin appeared a lighter shade green as well. Whether the differences were due to breeding or illness or something else entirely, she could not say. The beast grew a ragged beard upon its face, another unique feature for the type. Then she noticed its eyes.

Instead of the beady, pig-like eyes of a typical ogre, the giant's eyes shone in a distinctive green hue. Katja found herself under the intense scrutiny of that gaze. Was it about to devour her on the spot? She reached down for the stiletto.

The ogre leaned down so far that its face nearly touched her own. Its breath reeked of rotten meat. Her hand tightened on the handle of the blade.

The ogre's mouth parted.

"Woman," it said. "Mine."

Katja felt a flash of terror. How could it speak? Then she noticed the boots on its feet, the belt buckle holding up its filthy breeches. Part ogre. Part human.

"Woman," it said. "Mine."

She fainted.

Chapter Thirty-Two

"A dragon? Where?"

Thundar stared in the direction of Gerald's outstretched arm. Sure enough, a winged creature bore down on the royal party at high speed, the species impossible to distinguish due to glare from the sun but most certainly not a dragon owing to a vastly more primitive body shape, entirely lacking the smooth lines and sleek profile of a typical dragon.

"A dragon is coming," cried a woman.

"It's not a dragon," Thundar said.

Party guests ran screaming in all directions, followed by nannies, guards, and servants. Portly bodies jiggled with excess fat. Thundar ignored a deep-seated dragon instinct to give chase to fleeing prey and instead focused his attention on the incoming creature.

"Leave your axe at home, they said," Rogan shouted above the din. "It's just a picnic. What could possibly happen at a picnic?"

"The guards have betrayed the Emperor," Gerald said.

Thundar glanced over at the throne. Every last one of the Emperor's guards ran off, fleeing through the forest, abandoning their liege en masse. The Emperor remained seated, seemingly befuddled and uncomprehending. Zirac sat at the table still, the sorcerer's face hidden behind his hood. The Lady Gwendolyn rushed up to the Emperor's side and pulled on her father's hand in an apparent attempt to convince the man to take cover, but to no effect.

The flying creature hurled down through the sky, closing in like a demon from the abyss, not a dragon at all, Thundar saw—the fools!—but an oversized bat, a dragonbat, a nightmarish predator with a thick set of talons and canines capable of cutting a minor dragon in two with a single bite. Rather than descend on the Emperor, the bat's trajectory carried it on a direct course with Thundar's own table, or to be more precise, toward the wide-eyed Councilor Jones. Thundar drew a deep breath, stoking his internal fires to the maximum. Bring it on, he thought. Bring it on.

The bat swooped in. The Lady Gwendolyn's jeweled tiara flashed in the sun, sparkling and twinkling in a most fascinating manner, a temptation for the dragonbat that proved impossible to resist. The beast veered in the direction of the throne like a fish attracted to a piece of bait.

Rogan hollered yet another curse, but without his axe on hand, proved capable only of shouting and waving his arms. Councilor Jones kept seated in his chair as if frozen to the spot. Zirac's will snapped at last. Robes aflutter, the sorcerer fled in the direction of the castle. The Lady Gwendolyn draped her body atop the Emperor, shielding her father with her torso, and in so doing, exposing her unprotected spine to the sky. Thundar snarled at the tragedy about to unfold.

Like a hero out of a legend, Gerald leapt in front of the Lady Gwendolyn and swung a wooden stool in a mighty overhead blow. The stool splintered against the bat's skull with an impact that echoed among the trees. The beast crashed headfirst to the ground and tumbled through a series of high-speed cartwheels, and finally came to a rest a short distance away, wings broken, head bent back at an unnatural angle.

A strange calm followed. The few guests that still remained simply stood and stared. Nobody blew fire into the sky as a dragon would. Nobody so much as spoke a word. The wind whispered through the trees and the grass, but otherwise the unnatural silence continued. Thundar wondered if perhaps a witty comment might help the situation, something jovial and clever to be certain, but an uncharacteristically stern glance from Councilor Jones stayed the words in his throat.

The Lady Gwendolyn faced the dead bat for a long time before she turned back to Gerald and saturated the prince with stares of ultimate approval, her lips parted, eyes narrowed, bosom heaving. Gerald replied to her antics with a typically blank expression, saying nothing and doing nothing, just like some backwards hick from a swamp. Thundar shook his head: who taught social skills in North Bogsonia?

"It's a bat." Gerald nodded. "A dragonbat. We kill them back home when necessary, albeit not usually with a stool."

Gwendolyn grinned. The guests remained quiet.

"Nice party otherwise," Gerald added.

Gwendolyn shook back her hair. "You saved my life, and the life of my father as well. The guards fled, the councilors fled, nearly everyone fled but you. You are the bravest man in the entire Empire, bar none. You are a hero, both to the Empire and to myself personally."

Gerald nodded. "Glad I could help."

The picnickers broke into applause, slowly at first, then more quickly as the Lady Gwendolyn joined in. Gerald alone did not clap his hands, and judging from the pained expression on his face, appeared embarrassed by the sudden turn of events. Rogan added a series of piercing whistles to the applause. Councilor Jones beat his hands upon the table. Thundar blew a column of flame skyward.

The Emperor emerged from his stupor at long last, the slack-jawed expression replaced by a clear and penetrating gaze. He stood and faced the body of the giant bat. Even from where Thundar sat, the stench of the creature was overwhelming, reeking in death even worse than it had in life. The Emperor made no sign he even noticed the pungent smell as he placed his hand atop the Lady Gwendolyn's shoulder.

"You are unharmed?"

"Yes."

The Emperor scowled. "Where is my personal guard? Where are the other councilors?"

Gwendolyn scowled as well. "They betrayed you, abandoned you when you needed them most, all except for the valiant Prince Gerald of North Bogsonia. He killed this monster with little more than his bare hands and saved our lives. He alone you can trust."

The Emperor turned to Gerald. "How can I repay you for saving the life of my daughter?"

"It's okay, really," Gerald said.

"He's blowing it," Thundar whispered to Councilor Jones. "He should ask for the Lady Gwendolyn's hand in marriage."

"Quiet," came the councilor's reply.

"Have you no fear, my friend?" The Emperor said. "Not even of dragons?"

Gerald shrugged. "I knew it couldn't be a large dragon, as they're all dead. So I knew it must be something else."

"Yes, well said," the Emperor replied. "I'm glad to see that somebody kept their wits about them through all this."

Gerald nodded. "We're all relieved you are feeling better, Sire."

"Yes, feel a lot more like my old self now." The Emperor scratched his head. "Almost as if I were in a bit of a daze there earlier. Got all thick in the head or something."

"Thank goodness for Prince Gerald," the Lady Gwendolyn said. "Brave and handsome."

Thundar sat back in his chair. "This is actually going really well."

Councilor Jones pressed a finger against his lips as if shushing somebody.

"Yes, my dear, thank goodness is right," the Emperor said. "Prince Gerald, I require your services for a time. Do me a favor and put yourself at my disposal. I'd appreciate it. The Empire needs you."

"Of course, Sire."

Chapter Thirty-Three

Katja studied the war camp from the confines of a wooden cage.

A steady stream of ogres in full battle gear arrived in camp, and along with them came an assortment of wartime allies, goblins, trolls, minotaur, and others. Goblins roamed their designated sector of camp freely, but of the half-dozen rock trolls, which typically weighed over a ton with a brain the size of a peanut, none so much as moved a step without the attention of a bevy of handlers manipulating the chains attached to their stout necks.

A small group of minotaur kept to themselves along the far side of the camp, and in keeping with their reputation, limited their contact with the other races. Katja's previous notions about the beasts, derived solely from artists' renditions in story books, proved contrary to reality. From the neck down, the minotaur resembled human beings far more than did the bull-like animals portrayed in pictures, yet above the neck they looked completely bovine, their faces nearly indistinguishable from the old lady's milk cow back in Brookhaven.

And they were outcasts. Each minotaur was disfigured by a massive, spiraling brand that ran the entire length of the snout, tattooed from forehead to nostril. Whatever the nature of their crimes, branding followed by expulsion from the herd was known to be the harshest punishment in all of minotaur society. Of all species, none were more vain about their personal appearance. The transgressions of these particular individuals must have been particularly acute.

"It looks as if a full blown invasion of the Empire is about to take place," Katja said. "And here's the Emperor, about to disarm the population at large. It's almost enough to make me wonder which side he's on, that is, if I didn't already know Zirac was behind it. The carnage will be terrible unless we do something."

"What do you think they're keeping us alive for?"

Katja turned and stared.

The mountain woman did not wait for an answer. "Which one of us will first be its bride?"

"Are you losing your mind? Do not speak of it."

"You saw the way it looked at us. It called you its woman. You know what it intends."

"Then keep your eyes open for a way out of here. Unless you prefer the alternative."

The mountain woman paled. "I'd rather be eaten alive than suffer that fate."

"It'll never get to that. There are ways to make sure that such things do not happen. So calm your guts and steady your brain."

"Calm," the woman muttered. "Monsters out of a nightmare everywhere, and you say to be calm."

Katja nodded. "They have been too busy attending to war matters to get around to us yet, but our time will soon run out."

The mountain woman did not speak.

"Listen," Katja said. "It is terribly important that at least one of us escape from this place and puts out a warning. More important than our lives. So far as I know, nobody in Empire City has any idea the ogres are on the warpath. When I was a mercenary, the intelligence reports we heard from Smash described a scene of confusion and civil war, but the very existence of this army says something else entirely. Ogres are prone to bickering and internal fighting, but from what we have seen here so far, with the exception of a few lapses, they have learned a new discipline. I fear that Zirac is influencing the intelligence services and fixing the reports from Smash to suit his own agenda. Though what he'd gain from seeing the Empire laid to waste by an ogre army is beyond me."

"Who is Zirac?"

"A bad guy." Katka said. "Look, this bar on the cage is loose. It slides over a little bit when I push on it. After the sun goes down, then we'll make our break."

"They will give chase once they realize we are gone."

"Of course, but what of it? They will pursue us no matter when we escape. If we can find a stream or a river and hide our scent, then at least one of us might be able to get away."

"The goblins will still see well when it is dark. What about them?"

"They are not so many, and we will travel in the opposite direction from their encampment when we go. That big ogre left here this afternoon and has not yet returned. We may never have this chance again. Tonight is the right time."

"There's too many of them," the mountain woman said. "You will get caught."

"Stay here if you prefer," Katja said. "Experience the fate which you so abhor."

The sun dropped low, and dusk settled over the land. The ogres gathered around a bon fire in the middle of camp. Katja watched and waited, impatient to make a break for freedom, wondering all the while whether her captors, emboldened by the absence of their leader, might take the opportunity to consume their human guests. To her relief, the ogres ate from a cook pot set in the fire, slurping like starving pigs from trough-shaped plates.

A smallish ogre made its way over to the cage and placed within easy reach of the prisoners inside a pair of steaming bowls and two strips of sun dried meat. Katja refused to even look at the meat, the donor species might be human for all she knew, but a surprisingly appealing aroma wafted up from the contents of the bowls. The mountain woman snatched a bowl and held it up to her nose.

"What is it?" Katja said. "Something disgusting?"

The mountain woman looked surprised. "Cereal grain. Barley, I think."

Katja downed the contents of the other bowl in a couple of mouthfuls.

"Moo," she said.

"Is that supposed to be funny?"

Katja shrugged. "My mistake. Cows don't eat grain, do they? I think they eat grass. I should have clucked like a chicken. I jest because eating grain makes me feel like a farm animal."

The mountain woman shook her head and placed down the bowl.

"I can't eat it. Who knows what kind of horrible fertilizer they used to grow it?"

"They're ogres." Katja spoke slowly. "Not farmers. Ogres don't grow anything. The grain was stolen from somewhere."

"From where? You don't know for certain."

"I don't need to know the origin of the grain to be confident that it wasn't grown using human flesh for fertilizer."

Despite Katja's confident words, the grain churned uneasily in her stomach.

The moon climbed high into the sky, and still the ogre leader remained away from camp, an absence soon evident in the behavior of the other ogres. Rather than sharpen weapons and tend to armor as they had earlier, ogres stood around idly, chatting or casting dice. A cask made an appearance by the fire. A flurry of mugs drained the contents. Another cask. Katja bided her time, waiting for the perfect moment. A burst of shouted grunts and squeals announced the onset of the first major disagreement of the night.

Katja slammed her shoulder against the cage. The loose bar moved a fraction. She lifted back her leg and kicked out with her boot. The bar moved over another fraction. Alternating between teeth-rattling blows from her shoulder and sole-bruising kicks, she succeeded in creating a space between the bars nearly large enough to squeeze through.

"What are you doing?" The mountain woman grabbed Katja's arm. "You said we would wait until later tonight. When they sleep."

The shouts of ogres rang through the camp.

Katja pulled her arm free. "Now is the right time to go. They argue. They are distracted. We go now."

Katja forced her upper body between the bars of the cage, a squeeze so tight around her shoulders and chest that she felt the pressure might crush her ribs. Without warning, she slipped through up to her waist, leaving her dangling half in and half out of the cage, unable to touch the ground or to reach back and find purchase to push off. She squirmed and twisted.

"Push me through," she called.

Hands grabbed Katja's rump and shoved.

"Your behind is too big," the mountain woman said. "It's too wide."

"It is not. I just can't get in a decent position. Push harder."

Katja twisted and stretched and twisted some more.

"Too . . . big . . . ," the mountain woman complained.

"Almost . . . there . . . ." Katja popped free and fell in a heap on the ground.

The mountain woman stepped lithely between the bars and proceed to glance around like a frightened animal, eyes wide, legs shaking, clearly on the edge of panic. Down by the bon fire, negotiations between the quarreling ogres took a turn for the worse when one of a pair of freshly-separated combatants reached back his fist and struck his adversary a fresh blow across the side of the head, renewing the fistfight. While one small group of ogres shouted in an apparent attempt to regain the peace, a much larger crowd howled and waved their fists as if cheering on the spectacle.

"Do not just run off," Katja warned. "Come, let's move back out of the light of the fire. We will make our way around without being seen."

Not waiting to see if the mountain woman heard or even understood, Katja was on the move, creeping from one boulder to the next, each step taking her that much closer to freedom. A renewed resolve to put out a warning over the impending invasion of the Empire filled her heart, a yearning rooted in a desire to save as many lives as possible. Were the mountain woman recaptured, or to go missing, Katja would have no choice but to leave her behind.

The row between the ogres grew to a new pitch, followed by a sudden silence. Mugs clanked and angry voices turned cheery. Katja cursed the untimely truce, though a glance revealed that none of the beasts had yet ventured in the vicinity of empty cage. The mountain woman followed at a short distance, scurrying along at her own speed. Katja pressed on.

Moonlight bathed the land in a gentle glow, illuminating the path beneath Katja's feet. She veritably raced away from the ogre camp, willing her legs to greater speed despite the risk of a trip and fall.

The path led down a steep incline. The sound of rushing water filled her ears, and she leapt high in the air, sailing above the stream and barely breaking stride as she landed on the far bank. Exaltation filled her chest. She had escaped. The ogres would not catch her now.

She slammed face first against something hard and unyielding, stopping her in an instant in mid-stride. Before she could run or even so much as breathe, a huge hand wrapped around her hair and lifted her skyward.

"Woman." The giant half-ogre said. "Escape not."

Katja ignored the tearing sensation that accompanied dangling from her scalp as she reached down and withdrew the hidden stiletto, but before she could bring the blade into play, the ogre unexpectedly threw her to the ground. Of even greater surprise, the mutant beast dropped at her side, falling with a tremendous crash.

Katja scampered back to her feet. The mountain woman stood a few paces away, smiling broadly, a bloodstained rock the size of her head clasped in her hands.

"I sneak up on him," the mountain woman said.

The ogre moaned, thrashing its arms and legs, quickly regaining consciousness.

"I knew I could count on you." Katja lifted the stiletto. "This creature will pursue us if it is allowed to recover. Turn around if you don't like the sight of blood."

Chapter Thirty-Four

"The picnic was a great success," Thundar said. "You were really brave, Gerald, just like I knew you'd be. I had confidence in you right from the start."

"What start?" Gerald said. "What confidence? I acted as any man would. The Emperor was in danger, and so I did what I could to help. It was nothing more than my duty as a citizen."

Councilor Jones chuckled. "Your humble take on events hardly does your actions justice. You are the talk of the royal court for both saving the skin of the Emperor and attracting the notice of the fair Lady Gwendolyn. Rumors run wild, yet you seem unaware of it all."

"Really unaware," Thundar said. "Like just about the most unaware person in history."

"I'm aware," Gerald said. "I'm aware of everything. It's just that the very thought of getting involved with the royal family is a fool's game. How do you think Gwendolyn would enjoy living in Bogwood, you know, being so far away from family and friends?"

The councilor coughed into his hand. "A relationship with the princess would require her suitor to make Empire City his permanent home."

Gerald nodded. "And spending the remainder of my days stuck in Empire City is just the start of it."

A servant entered the room at a dead run.

"What is it?" Councilor Jones said.

"A royal messenger has arrived. He demands to speak with your esteemed guest."

"Which esteemed guest?" Councilor Jones smiled. "Does he seek Thundar, the dragon?"

Thundar flapped his wings.

"No," the servant said. "Rather, the royal messenger requests a word with the esteemed Prince Gerald."

"Oh." The councilor winked in Thundar's direction. "Show him in."

"You're going to miss your big chance, Gerald," Thundar said. "You should pursue the princess while you still have the chance. You make her wings stiff. Take it from me, dragons are lucky in love."

"Your own mate left you and flew away," Gerald said. "You call that lucky in love?"

"Yes," Thundar said. "Otherwise, I'd be with her to this day, stuck in a sham of a marriage like Rogan."

Rogan scowled.

"No offense," Thundar added. "But that vulture of a mate of mine sailing off into the sunset turned out to be the sweetest updraft to ever come my way. Look at me now, a guest in the home of a friend of the Emperor, and a friend to another man who's destined to inherit the throne, be it through marriage."

Gerald shook his head. "Sorry, but I'm not about to marry anyone."

The house servant returned with the royal messenger in tow.

"A message from his excellency," the messenger announced, "addressed to one Prince Gerald of North Bogsonia."

"I am he."

The messenger produced a rolled parchment tied with a bright red ribbon. He pulled away the ribbon with a grand flourish and yanked open the scroll in a single exaggerated motion.

"Prince Gerald is invited to attend the royal banquet in celebration of the fifth anniversary of the Lady Gwendolyn's coming out, in two days hence."

"Another banquet." Gerald sighed. "Councilor, didn't you say that the royal picnic we just attended was the last public event of the season?"

"And so it was," the councilor said. "The Lady Gwendolyn's coming out is a private affair. Only a select few are invited to her private functions, unlike public events, where all nobles are expected to attend."

"Oh." Gerald said something unintelligible.

"What was that?" Thundar said. "Speak up, I couldn't hear you."

"I said that I see. That I understand." Gerald spoke as if irritated. "I was supposed to be heading back home right about now. That isn't about to happen from the looks of things."

"One does not refuse a personal invitation by the Emperor," Councilor Jones said. "I hope you are not considering rebuffing the princess's request?"

"Not at all. My concern is only that Bogwood is far away, and the season is growing later every day. If we don't leave soon, there's a chance of being caught on the wrong side of the mountains when winter comes. Then we won't make it back home until springtime."

The councilor waved his hand dismissively. "You should still have several weeks before the risk of snowfall blocking the pass becomes acute."

"There's no rush," Rogan said. "Even if we do spend the winter here, it's no big deal."

"The invitation is extended to include a second individual as well," the messenger said. "One master Thundar by name."

Thundar flapped his wings so hard that he nearly lifted off the ground.

"That was Gwendolyn's doing. She really likes me."

"That's the extent of the invite?" Parrot asked. "There's nothing in there about Prince Gerald's personal chronicler attending? The official record of North Bogsonia would benefit from my presence."

The messenger shook his head. "The invitation mentions only the two individuals already named."

"Not even myself?" Councilor Jones said.

"No, sir. Only the two individuals already named."

"Young dragon, you are in exclusive company," Councilor Jones said.

"I'll behave myself," Thundar promised. "I won't try to move in on Gerald's woman if that's what you're getting at."

Councilor Jones smiled. "Yes, that's exactly what I was getting at."

Chapter Thirty-Five

Thundar's stomach rumbled unhappily, and still there remained no sign of the promised food.

"No," Gerald said in response to the Emperor's question. "I'm not betrothed to be married back home. We choose our own brides in North Bogsonia."

The Lady Gwendolyn smiled until most of her teeth showed.

At long last, servants carried trays of food up to the royal dinner table, each dish an exquisite creation. Roast duck, flambe chicken, pork chops, charbroiled mutton, the smells were such that a string of drool slid from Thundar's mouth and hung suspended in the air, swinging back and forth like a rope, until he remembered to wipe the offensive matter away.

"Most nearly all Imperial unions are political in nature." The Emperor prattled on as if unaware of the arrival of the food. "That is, marriages are arranged with one eye on political or military gain, if not both eyes." He chuckled. "But once in a long while, even those considerations are secondary, such as when the stability of the very Empire is at stake."

Gerald nodded. "Ruling must be difficult."

Thundar shook his head: unless the Emperor got his act together and ordered the food served up, the servants were only going to stand around indefinitely, the food steaming away until it all went cold, the guests going hungry until they starved, even if the only guests in sight were himself and Gerald. Something was seriously wrong when the consumption of food at mealtime took on less importance than did endless blather.

"Difficult indeed." The Emperor slammed his fist against the opposite palm. "The noble houses would rather see the Empire fall into anarchy than watch someone they disapprove of ascend to the crown. They all harbor delusions that they themselves might emerge in a position of power following a period of civil strife. The truth is that everyone loses in such a situation."

"Absolutely," Gerald said. "Civil war needs to be avoided at all costs."

"I concur," Thundar said.

The Emperor smiled. "How is courtship carried our among dragons, Thundar? Do dragons complicate the matter as much as we humans do?"

Thundar cleared his throat. "In Dragonden, when a young male dragon sets his sights on an eligible female dragon, he dons his best armor and seeks to strike up a conversation with her. Best if he's suave. Brings gifts and the like." He stared meaningfully at Gerald. "He talks to the female, instead of just sitting there like a sucker." He looked back at the Emperor. "The clutch of eggs comes later."

"But that's how regular citizens are married," Gwendolyn said. "Men and women get together based on how well they like one another. Unfortunately, the situation is less straightforward for members of royalty."

Thundar nodded. "Dragons are a casual people, if widely misunderstood. Ah, I see the food has arrived. Excellent."

"It seems that fully half of my subjects are misunderstood," the Emperor muttered. "Or so they tell me."

A servant from the Emperor's personal retinue approached the table.

"What is it?" the Emperor said.

"Sire, I beg your pardon, but Zirac, requests a word. He says it is urgent."

"Send him right in."

The magician entered the room in a rush. Only his pointy nose and chin jutted beyond the rim of his upturned hood. He carried a parchment in one hand.

"My apologies for interrupting dinner, Sire," Zirac said. "But the calligraphers have finished their work on the order proclaiming my humble self as the new head of the intelligence bureau. As the welfare of the Empire is at stake, I saw no reason to delay seeking out your notarization on this bill."

The Emperor frowned, shaking his head.

"I never . . . ."

Thundar watched in amazement as the most extreme change came over the Emperor. The man's penetrating gaze took on a distant look, as if staring at an object in the distance that he alone could see. His face, animated with emotion and alive with humor the moment before, slackened to become zombielike, seemingly devoid of thought or feeling of any kind.

"The bill, Sire." Zirac held out the parchment.

"Yes, of course." The Emperor held out his hand.

Zirac smiled.

"Have this mage arrested, Gwendolyn," Gerald said. "He has drugged your father."

Gwendolyn sat very still. The guards grabbed the hilts of their swords.

Zirac laughed long and mockingly. "What kind of stupidity is this you swamp pig? You are a fool. Go back to the swamp where you came from."

Gwendolyn blanched.

"Don't worry, princess," Gerald said. "I'll break his neck before he can cast a spell."

"Are you insane?" Zirac snarled.

"What about this matter of drugging?" Gwendolyn said. "You have proof? Granted, my father has been acting stupefied whenever this mage comes into his presence as of late. But you know something for certain?"

Gerald nodded. "The Emperor carries the musk of a certain medicinal plant."

"It's a health balm," Gwendolyn said. "Given to him by Zirac."

"A gift," the magician explained.

"At first I couldn't place the smell," Gerald said. "There are countless plants in the swamp, and many carry a distinct odor. But then I caught a whiff of Zirac. He also carries a musk, but a different one. And then I knew."

"Ridiculous," Zirac said. "I provided the Emperor a balm that relaxes both mind and body."

"Then you knew what, Gerald?" Gwendolyn said.

"The source of the balm," Gerald said. "In the deepest swamps, there grows a carnivorous scourge known as the skullweed fern. The stems from the plant contain an aromatic sap that, once exposed to the milky fluid in the roots, produces a vapor which makes any person who breathes it extremely susceptible to suggestion. It is a narcotic."

Gwendolyn looked shocked. "You mean . . . ?"

"I mean this wizard gave the Emperor one half of the drug in the balm," Gerald said. "He is wearing the other half."

A bead of sweat rolled off Zirac's chin and fell on the floor at his feet.

"Ridiculous," the mage said. "All lies."

"Are you sure, Gerald?" Gwendolyn said. "Father, can you hear me?"

"Hear you, yes," the Emperor said. "Hear."

"He's not all there," Gwendolyn said.

"Tell Zirac to go stand in a corner," Gerald said. "Anywhere that's not within breathing range. The Emperor will come around after a while."

"See here," Zirac said. "I will not be treated like some sort of criminal."

"Magician," Gwendolyn said. "You will do as you are told. Guards, escort Zirac to the hallway and keep him under watch until you are ordered to return."

"You are all fools," Zirac hollered. "What do you think you're doing? Unhand me."

A pack of grinning guards descended on the magician and dragged him bodily from the room, their efficiency such that Zirac's feet barely touched the ground. The mage's protests grew quiet in the distance.

"Father?" Gwendolyn said. "Oh, he's the same as before."

"Give it a few moments. The bad air needs to work its way out of his body."

The Emperor blinked and snorted and even drooled a little, but like a man waking from a dream, awareness returned to his eyes.

"Who?" the Emperor said. "What's going on here? What happened? Gwendolyn? Have I been asleep?"

"Good job, Gerald," Thundar said.

"What?" The Emperor said. "Who?"

"Sit easy, father," Gwendolyn said. "His name is Gerald the Magnificent. And we are safe now."

Chapter Thirty-Six

Zirac screamed in rage.

Rare and irreplaceable glass and ceramic vessels shattered into fragments against the tower wall. He spared nothing, flinging flask, bottle, beaker, and urn with equal fury. The jar containing the misshapen remains of his old magical rival found its way into his hand and burst against the floor. The clawed thing within writhed and died, freed from its torment at long last, a loss that represented but a mere sidebar to the disasters of the day.

Banned. He was banned from Empire City on pain of death, forever expelled to Wizardhome. All his plans for naught. A lifetime of scheming and manipulating and risk gone in a single moment. And to add insult to injury, the villain responsible for the catastrophe had been announced by the Emperor as betrothed to the Lady Gwendolyn.

He hurled an ancient chalice against the wall, freeing a disembodied spirit that went racing around the room, and howling so maniacally as to vibrate the very stones underfoot. Zirac lifted his hand and spoke a minor spell, shooing the thing away before it flew dangerously close.

His decision to break up the dinner party seemed like the obvious course of action at the time. How could he have known the Bogsonian's knowledge of exotic flora rivaled the experience of any expert? Or that Zirac's new poisons and potions happened to grow in the yokel's own backyard? The irony struck him as nearly to much to bear.

He made his way over to the window and gazed down on Empire City. Citizens walked the streets in large numbers, scurrying in and out of shops, sitting on park benches, engaged in wasting their time on personal matters rather than serving the needs and wants of their betters. He shook his head in disgust and walked back to his desk and cast a spell of Summoning.

A raven landed on the windowsill moments later.

"Master," the bird croaked.

"Fly eastward in all haste," Zirac commanded. "Find the ogre commander, Betzkil. He is ordered to begin the invasion at once. Scorched earth policy applies. Total destruction. Go."

"As you command." The raven spread its wings and disappeared amid a flutter of feathers.

Zirac felt a trifle less depressed imagining the panic would sweep Empire City when word arrived of yet another invasion of the Empire. Screaming in the streets. Food hoarding. Flight. And above all, anger directed toward the Emperor over the unprepared state of the military, rage at the breakdown in intelligence that allowed an invasion force to assemble on the very doorstep of the Empire without anyone's knowledge. Voices would call for regime change, he would see to it personally. An arrow in the Emperor's back delivered by a dastardly ogre assassin would guarantee a long-overdue change in leadership, the obvious successor being the individual who had just saved the kingdom from destruction.

But first, there was yet another problem to deal with.

"Waif."

The shadow creature floated near Zirac's desk.

"Contact the assassin's guild. I require their services immediately. Price and client will be discussed once they arrive."

The waif shimmered in a silver glow. "They refuse your invitation. They will not come to the tower. Their master states that they still await the return of their colleague from the last meeting at the tower."

Zirac sought to control his anger. "Fine, then tell them to meet me at my office at the castle. I must return there once more to clean out my things before I supposedly relinquish the chambers."

"They will arrive in the guise of merchants."

"What else would they do, come dressed as assassins?" Zirac took a deep breath. Show some patience for now, he coached himself. Vent on these fools later, starting with the guilds. "Tell them to meet me at the castle thusly."

Zirac descended the stairs and stepped outside the tower. The wind howled and rain fell on the cobblestones. He hurried across the open courtyard to the main castle keep, moving as quickly as possible. The sensation of water on his skin sent a shiver of disgust down his spine, urine from the gods as it were. Why did it have to rain the one day he left the tower? And why did the Lady Gwendolyn act like a cheap harlot in the presence of the Bogsonian fool, fluttering her eyelids like she had a disease of the eyeballs? Her shallow nature on top of her immaturity struck him as particularly galling.

A pair of guards stood duty beside a side door leading to the castle, and as Zirac walked past, one of the guards laughed, a long, derisive snicker, ugly and mocking. Scathing.

Zirac nearly came to a stop, stunned by the lack of respect. That the word of his banishment to Wizardhome had already circulated through the troops, there could be no doubt. He clenched his teeth and continued on, back straight, head up, pride undaunted by the rudeness of primates. Of course, such a display of insolence beggared the most painful death ever witnessed by the gods, and the guards would soon get exactly what was coming to them. One thing at a time, he decided: first, meet with the assassins. Then kidnap the princess.

Pug glanced through the kitchen window and spotted Zirac tromping across the courtyard, the mage approaching the castle despite his banishment to Wizardhome. That the serving staff would be happy to see the last of the smelly sorcerer was the understatement of the year, but opinion remained evenly split as to whether he would leave peacefully or attempt to bring disaster down upon their heads first.

Pug wrung his hands together, wracked by indecision. Katja's fate preyed on his mind every single day. Was she even still alive? Captured and jailed? Did the authorities have any idea of her whereabouts? Not since she disappeared from the crypt had he last heard her name mentioned, and only then by a guard speculating on her whereabouts.

With the ease of long practice, Pug entered the service corridor and shuffled through the darkness. A thin beam of light shone across the corridor at the spy hole leading to Zirac's chambers. Pug held his breath and peered into the room.

Empty. He licked his lips and found his tongue to be dry.

The door to Zirac's chambers opened. A trio of men entered the room, the mage and two others whom Pug did not recognize, merchants judging from their garb. The wizard waved his hands in strange patterns and spoke the incomprehensible chantings of a magic spell.

"Nobody can hear us now, not even a fly on the wall."

Once again, the magician's words carried clearly to Pug, as if he were being personally addressed.

"You are fortunate that we came." The merchant spoke in a harsh tone. "After our brother went missing, there was a debate over your fate."

Pug felt a shock of surprise: whatever the man's dress, he was no mere shopkeeper to be talking so to Zirac.

Zirac only shrugged. "Do not cast blame on me that you cannot trust your so-called brother. That he fled with the loot. The man was paid in full, and you know it. The waif is my witness."

"The waif," the man said, "is not here to protect you."

"Think you that I have no other defenses?" Zirac sneered. "Anyone so foolish as to attack me would find out soon enough."

"I tire of this conversation," said the man. "What do you want?"

"The usual. Tomorrow. Your client will arrive at the old teamster station around noon. You remember the spot?"

The man nodded. "Where we harvested internal organs from those vagrants for your experiments?"

"That's the one. You should be in place and ready to do the job slightly before noon. I intend to be there myself. I will be in the company of a certain guest who will do well to witness the event."

The false merchant shook his head. "There can be no witnesses to our work, have you forgotten?"

"Nonsense," Zirac said. "The guest is a woman. She will come straight back to my tower afterwards and stay there for the rest of her life and very likely for much longer. She is to be taught a lesson in reality, that a certain young man whom she adores will never come to her rescue."

"So long as she remains solely your responsibility. We require the standard fee."

"Of course."

"Paid up front."

Zirac scoffed. "You don't trust me?"

The fake merchant snorted. "For the sake of everyone involved, a new policy at the guild requires that all fees be paid up front and in full. That way, none need to come back later and collect."

Zirac laughed.

Chapter Thirty-Seven

"Chronicler, I'm going down to the Drunken Sow for a mug," Rogan announced. "Care to join me?"

Parrot looked up from scribbling on a parchment. "Yes, don't mind if I do. Prince Gerald is engaged with the royal groomers until later this morning. There isn't much chronicling to be done at the moment."

"Bring money," Rogan said. "Counselor, are you in?"

"It's kind of early for me. The Drunken Sow you say? That's a squalid dive, isn't it? It was the last time I had business in the old part of town."

Rogan nodded. "Down to earth people there, folksy clientele, that's part of the charm."

The shortest route to the pub led past a large teamster station. Wagons of all shapes and sizes crowded the dusty roadway in front of the barn-like building, with passengers and drivers alike held up from reaching their final destination by a bevy of tax collectors and contraband officials. Rogan maneuvered carefully between mounds of horse dung on the road, the stench thick in his nostrils, and hurried through the weatherbeaten front door of the Drunken Sow Inn.

"What a dump," Parrot said. "The councilor was right."

"She's old school." Rogan paused just inside the doorway to allow his eyes to adjust to the shaded interior. Parrot made his way to a table near the back of the pub. Rogan dropped down on a stool along the opposite side of the table.

"It'll be nice to get back home." Parrot said.

Rogan shrugged. "The way I see it, if the Emperor decides to keep us here until the snow flies and we don't make it back until next year, then so be it. There's not much I can do about it in any case."

The innkeeper arrived at the table. Rogan ordered a bucket of ale and two mugs. Parrot handed over the appropriate number of coins. Rogan shifted his weight so that the handle of his axe hung off to his side rather than ride up on his stool and press against his spine. The innkeeper returned with the requested beverages. Rogan took a long sip of the golden liquid. He smacked his lips.

"Why did you bring your weapon?" Parrot asked. "Expecting trouble?"

"You never know. Don't forget the Emperor's picnic. I won't be caught without my axe again."

"The Lady Gwendolyn has taken a liking to Prince Gerald," Parrot said. "I think it's now an open question as to when we're leaving."

Rogan drank long and deep before responding. "As I've said, whatever happens is alright with me. I'm so devoted to the Empire that my personal wants and needs are as nothing. I'm that dedicated. Well?"

"Well, what?"

"How come you're not writing any of this down? About my loyalty?"

"You're making a common error," Parrot said. "No individual can write their own historical legacy, not in any meaningful way. Many are the instances where even the rulers of large kingdoms went to great lengths to promote their own self-serving version of events in place of historical truth, but their manipulations are transparent in the end."

Rogan snorted. "Then it's good for me I'm not the ruler of a kingdom. But you didn't answer my question. Why didn't you write down what I said about serving the Empire?"

"I just explained, if you were listening."

"It'll make me look like a liar."

Parrot shrugged. "Immodest, perhaps."

Rogan frowned. "This pitcher is empty."

"Already?"

"I'll go get us another," Rogan said. "I'm guessing this innkeeper won't be back for some time, and I'm getting dehydrated."

Rogan strolled up to the massive, engraved wood bar set in the corner of the pub, empty jug in hand. The front door flung open and a tall individual entered the Drunken Sow at a rapid walk. Whether from inattention or because of the sudden shift from bright sunlight outside to the gloom of the pub, the newcomer ran straight into Rogan, grunting as he bounced back. His eyes narrowed to slits and then he was on his way again, speeding around Rogan and passing through a doorway at the far end of the pub. The innkeeper refilled Rogan's pitcher from a spigot attached to a wooden barrel.

"What's in that room?" Rogan asked. "The one on the end where that guy just went?"

"Rooms for our guests," said the innkeeper. "In case you haven't noticed, this is an inn as well as a pub."

"Been busy around here lately, what with the Emperor's birthday and all?"

"Sure. Busy enough."

"Do your guests usually stay for only a night or two? Or for longer?"

The innkeeper frowned. "What's with all the questions?"

"I'd like to open a place like this when I retire from soldiering," Rogan said. "I'm curious about the type of clientele I could expect. Mostly short stays?"

The innkeeper nodded. "Some short, some longer. You should buy this place. I'm willing to sell. The lifestyle of an innkeeper is awesome."

"I'm listening. How about that last guy that just came in here? When did he first come around?"

"I'd need to check my records to be certain, but I think he's been here for a couple of weeks. But that's privileged information."

"He gave me quite a look when we bumped."

"I don't doubt it," the innkeeper said. "He's not a very friendly sort, neither him nor his friend. I don't know what they're about and truth be told, I don't care, just so long as they pay their keep and don't bring no trouble around here."

"Are most of your guests of a friendlier variety?"

"They are. Seriously, you should buy this place. You'll get rich."

The door at the end of the pub banged open. The stranger sped back through the pub, making a beeline for the front door at high speed. A bulge beneath his robe jutted out from his side.

Rogan hurried back to his table. "I need to go check on something."

"Now?" Parrot said. "You just bought a pail of ale."

"The guy that just came through here has a tattoo on his forearm. I saw it when we knocked heads and his sleeve came up. It's the image of a bloody dagger and a skeletal hand gripping the handle."

"An assassin?" Parrot said. "Are you sure?"

Rogan shrugged. "I only saw the ink for a moment, but it was enough."

"Why would an assassin stay at an inn?" Parrot said. "Wouldn't the local assassin's guild have a clubhouse or some such?"

"Assassins aren't exactly welcome where they operate," Rogan said. "They don't have headquarters like your regular guilds do. They move their guys around, usually after they make a hit or are preparing for one. Red and Skunk were slaughtered like sheep, and that feat wasn't accomplished by just anyone. Those boys were good soldiers. The innkeeper told me that this guy and his buddy have been here for a couple of weeks, which puts the timing about right for the hit on Red and Skunk. It's a long shot, but I'm going to follow him and and see what he's up to."

Rogan hurried out through the door to the street. The chronicler followed.

"You must be serious," Parrot said. "I never thought I'd live to see the day when you left behind a full pitcher of ale."

"You should have brought it along." Rogan spotted the assassin turning down a side street: a few more seconds of delay, and they would have lost track of him altogether. "Chasing down killers is thirsty business."

Chapter Thirty-Eight

Gerald read the ransom note printed on a scrap of parchment.

"The Lady Gwendolyn has been abducted."

"What?" Councilor Jones turned pale atop his couch. "Kidnapped? Is this a bad joke? Who would dare?"

Gerald held up the note. "I'm guessing it's the same person who tied this parchment to that raven's leg and trained it to fly here."

The councilor stuttered and stammered before his voice engaged.

"Is the kidnapper insane? Wait until the Emperor hears! He will leave no stone unturned across the entire Empire to get his beloved daughter back. The army will—"

"No," Gerald said. "This note makes clear the kidnapper will kill the princess if I notify the authorities. I must meet with her abductor alone."

Councilor Jones rose to his feet. "The army is about to be turned out in force anyhow. The absence of the princess will not go unnoticed for long."

As if on cue, a servant entered the room.

"Master, soldiers are here. They demand to speak with you. They say it is an emergency."

"Show them in immediately."

A captain in the Emperor's army marched into the room. His expression reflected equal parts anger and grief.

Councilor Jones rose to his feet. "Captain, what can I do for you?"

"There is a problem at the castle. It appears that the Lady Gwendolyn went missing sometime last night."

Councilor Jones gaped. "No."

"Yes, as incredible as it sounds."

"How do you mean she went missing?" Gerald said. "Did she just up and leave without anyone noticing? She went sleepwalking and got lost?"

"We don't know," the soldier said. "The consensus is that she was likely kidnapped. The Emperor demands that we establish communication with whoever is responsible, but so far our efforts have went nowhere."

"I'm astounded," Councilor Jones said. "What kind of security do they have at the castle where the daughter of the Emperor can be snatched like a commoner's sheep?"

The soldier shook his head. "We do not know yet how it happened. The Lady Gwendolyn's personal maids report falling into an unnaturally deep sleep. When they woke, the princess was gone. The guards stationed outside the chambers noticed nothing out of the ordinary. The Emperor ordered the royal consort to be informed of what has transpired as a courtesy."

"I appreciate the courtesy," Gerald said.

"How can we help?" Councilor Jones asked.

"The Emperor asks that every loyal citizen devote all of his or her resources to locating the princess, that they search every nook, cranny, and outbuilding on their respective holdings for any sign of the Lady Gwendolyn."

"Of course." Councilor Jones beckoned with a hand. A servant ran out of the room.

"The order has been given. Anything else?"

The guard shook his head. "Nothing else you can do. You will be notified of events as the search continues."

The servants escorted the soldier from the room.

"I'd best get ready," Gerald said.

"You're still set on this course?" Councilor Jones said. "You're determined to confront the Lady Gwendolyn's abductor all by yourself?"

"That's what the note demands."

"What other choice do we have?" Thundar said. "But make no mistake about it, Councilor Jones, if it's a fight someone wants, then it's a fight we'll give him."

"You're not coming," Gerald said.

"Again, I must protest," Councilor Jones said. "There is only one possible reason to include the stipulation you come alone, and that is because it's a trap. Otherwise the kidnapper would simply demand that you deliver a large ransom to secure her release. You'll be killed for certain."

"What do you mean I'm not coming?" Thundar said. "You need me."

"It's safer for you here," Gerald said. "And the princess will be killed for certain if I don't do as the kidnapper demands. I can defend myself in a fight if it comes down to it."

"How will you defend against an arrow in your back?" Councilor Jones said. "Against a group of heavily armed men? I understand the anguish you must feel for the safety of your future bride, but don't be foolish. I will send a squad of guards to trail you."

"No," Gerald said. "The kidnapper might well be watching for such trickery and kill Gwendolyn in retaliation. My only chance of getting her back in one piece is to meet the fiend on his own terms and wait for an opportunity to turn the tables."

"I cannot warn you against this plan strongly enough."

Gerald shrugged. "Be that as it may, I cannot sit around here while Gwendolyn is flayed alive because I refused a meeting."

The councilor rubbed his jaw. "When you put it that way . . . ."

Gerald stared at the ransom note. "The old teamster station is the meeting place. Where can I find it?"

Pug scurried down the hallway, redoubling his steps as he rounded a corner—and very nearly stepped on an overweight mini-dragon coming in the opposite direction. Only a last moment shuffle of his feet prevented his sandals from slamming the plump creature flat against the flagstones.

"Sorry," he called back reflexively.

"No problem," the dragon said.

Pug pressed on for another half-dozen paces before coming to a stop.

"Excuse me, but I am in dire need of assistance."

The dragon tipped back its little helmet. "Then you're talking to the right dragon. How are you in need?"

"It's a long story." Pug suddenly had no idea where to begin. "But the gist of it is that I overheard Zirac the mage planning to do something that isn't very nice, and to do it to a woman at that."

"Do what? To what woman?"

"I don't know for sure," Pug said. "He never said her name."

The dragon spread its wings. "Hold nothing back, for I am Thundar, Master of the Barrel Roll, Devourer of Cities. Dragons see through lies like a maiden spots a rake's false promises."

"Truly?"

The dragon peeled back its lips, exposing a mouthful of teeth.

"Not really, but you'd be surprised how often repeating that line encourages people to tell the truth."

"The Princess Gwendolyn was kidnapped last night," Pug said.

"That's no secret. Everyone is looking for her."

"I overheard Zirac say he plans to take a woman to his tower. He intends to take her there whether she likes it or not."

"And you think this woman is the Lady Gwendolyn?" The dragon's eyes widened. "You must tell the Emperor immediately, the guards, everyone."

"I don't know for sure it's her. I don't even know if he's really even planning anything, not for certain. You had to hear the conversation. My telling the Emperor what I heard would involve admitting I was listening in on the private conversations of castle guests rather than carrying out my duties of a servant, a firing offense. Nobles have a lot of stuff they don't want anyone to know about. I might get thrown into prison for accidentally overhearing them."

"Normally I'd ask Prince Gerald what to do," the dragon said. "But he's gone on a mission. I was too unpredictable to bring along, too much of a wildcard. Councilor Jones isn't around either, he's out searching for Gwendolyn. My other friends went to a pub this morning. Other than a random guard, I don't know who you should talk to. What about the head of your order?"

"Master Thespus would be no help," Pug said. "He's just like the others. I'd be thrown in the lockup the moment I admitted to overhearing our guests. Eavesdropping is strictly forbidden in my line of work. Of course, I was acting only in the best interests of the realm."

"Of course," Thundar said. "It sounds to me like you need to take matters in your own hands. That's what a dragon would do. What's your plan for action?"

Pug frowned. "I thought I'd tell somebody about the problem and let them deal with it. That's a kind of an action."

"And a wise action, under normal circumstances," the dragon said. "One of my favorites, in fact. But what about now?"

"I don't know," Pug said. "We could walk over to Zirac's tower and see what happens."

The dragon snorted. Little flames shot from its nostrils.

"You intend to break into the magician's tower? Wizards have magical defenses guarding their belongings, spirits, ghosts, and the like."

"I never said we should force our way inside the tower," Pug said. "Maybe we could just hang around outside, hide ourselves as best we can and watch and wait. If we see that Zirac is up to something ghastly, we can alert the guards."

"Wait for something to happen." The dragon nodded. "A worthy plan, especially when stuck for a better one. The only idea I like even more is if we were to change the locks on the tower door and leave Zirac standing outside in the rain, watch him screaming spells until he's finally forced to blow the door off its hinges. That'd be a sight to remember, but I doubt we can pull it off."

"Should we try?"

"Not right away," the dragon said. "Watch and wait is my counsel, at least until we get bored."

Chapter Thirty-Nine

"Show yourself, Zirac. Let's have this out."

Gerald's words faded away to nothing among the remains of the old teamster station. The roof of the building had long since fallen in, the walls flat on the ground or missing altogether. The charred remnants of multiple campfires spotted the area. Refuse and rotten timbers lay scattered about. Thistle and mustard weed grew in dense patches of green.

"Cowardly mage. Hiding behind a woman."

Two men in identical black tunics stepped out from behind a mound of dirt. They held naked swords and wore no visible armor. Hoods concealed their faces.

"Did you bring the princess?" Gerald called. "I'm ready to take her off your hands."

The men advanced on Gerald in perfect tandem, precise and silent, catlike on booted feet.

Gerald slid his sword free from the scabbard on his hip. "Too bad it wasn't me you two clowns surprised in the jakes that night. We would have ended this then and there, but better late than never. Come and get it."

The assassins closed in without speaking a word. Gerald shuffled to his right side, lifted his sword, and feigned a lunge at the nearest man, seeking to maneuver his adversaries one behind the other and render their numerical advantage mute if only but for a moment. Inconveniently, the first assassin faded back while the other began to circle around to Gerald's rear and come upon him from behind. Gerald decided that a change in tactics was in order. He turned tail and ran.

The assassins gave chase.

Gerald sprinted down a winding path, willing his feet to move faster every step of the way. Heaps of garbage and dense thickets blocked his intended path to the street, and so he turned in the opposite direction and charged between a jumble of building blocks. A wild hope sprang up in his heart, an expectation that perhaps he might somehow have managed to throw off his pursuers. A quick look back revealed that the assassins had closed to about twenty paces, a gap growing narrower by the moment.

Gerald poured on all possible speed rounding a sharp bend. A patch of thistle provided the only cover in sight. He jumped back among the dark green stalks and crouched low. Footsteps approached at a dead run. He ripped his sword through a mighty blow, but rather than the sweet sensation of iron hewing through flesh and bone, the blade clanged off another sword, leaving him to wonder for a brief instant whether his intended target possessed a superior set of reflexes compared to most men or simply had gotten lucky. Then Gerald was running again, the assassins hot on his heels.

Footprints stood out in the sand that Gerald recognized as his own. He was back to the spot where the chase started, except that now his chest ached with fatigue and his legs felt rubbery from exertion. Tactics swirled through his mind, each in turn discarded as impractical or misguided. There seemed no getting around taking on the pair of killers at the same time, a daunting task from which to emerge alive.

A rustle in the nearby bushes preceded the arrival of a second pair of men on the scene. Gerald blinked in astonishment.

"Rogan? Parrot?"

"I knew it." Rogan waved his axe threateningly. "I knew that guy was up to no good. Care for some assistance, my prince?"

"Yes. Talk about good timing. How did you know to come here?"

The assassins squared off against Gerald and Rogan individually.

"I met this one in a pub." Rogan jabbed his axe in the direction of the man facing him. "I think it was this one. Anyway, he has a tattoo on his arm announcing his occupation. Talk about smart. Takes a real brainy guy to announce to the world that he's an assassin."

The assassin's sword blurred through a wicked arc. Rogan grinned as he deflected the blow aside. The assassin attacked again, his blade a tapestry of flashing metal, thrusting and slashing in a frenzy nearly too fast for the human eye to follow. Rogan swung his axe. The assassin's head tumbled into the dirt, and in a show for the ages, the corpse remained standing for long moments, spraying great gouts of blood and gore skyward. One arm lifted spasmodically, shaking and twitching, a headless ghoul from a children's story, and it finally collapsed, shuddered, and went still.

The other assassin chopped a blow aimed at Gerald's legs but at the last possible moment switched to a double-handed thrust. Gerald stepped aside and watched as the blade slid past his shoulder. The assassin stumbled forward. Rogan swung his axe. The head of the second assassin rolled into the dirt. The corpse fell as if struck by lightning.

"No dance this time?" Rogan kicked the severed head, sending it sailing through the air. "I guess not."

"Impressive," Parrot said. "You swing that axe as if it were a feather."

"That's why men call me axe slayer."

Parrot scrawled on a parchment. "Duly noted."

A woman's scream rent the air.

Gerald turned and spotted Zirac running back toward the road, the mage staggering as he fled, a struggling captive in his arms. He forced his prisoner within a horse-drawn carriage, slammed shut the door, and hopped atop the driver's seat. A single flick of the long carriage reins, and the horses charged off to a rumble of thundering hooves.

Gerald ran in pursuit, his vision gone red with rage. Rogan kept pace at his side. Despite their efforts, only a cloud of dust remained of the wagon and its occupants by the time they reached the road.

"Zirac must have gone mad." Rogan spoke between panting breaths. "What does he think he's doing taking the princess prisoner?"

"Come on." Gerald set off at a dead run down the street. "We won't be able to catch the carriage, but if we're quick about it, maybe we can keep on the dust trail."

"Where do you think he's taking her?" Rogan said.

"Probably back to his tower," Gerald called over his shoulder. "It's just about the only place he has left."

"Should we be doing this?" Thundar said.

Zirac's tower reached high into the sky, looking every bit the part of an evil sorcerer's den. Grim and foreboding. Ancient and sinister. A narrow door at the base of the structure and a small window directly beneath the battlements on the roof marred the otherwise featureless cylinder of gray brickwork, a home that only an eagle or a magician could love.

"Should we be doing what?" Pug said.

"Standing here in plain view. Right out in the open like this. It's not what we predators normally do."

"Where are we going to hide?" Pug said.

Thundar glanced around the castle grounds, noting the manicured lawns, the flowerbeds, the cobblestone pathways, and the carefully trimmed hedges. The excess of decorative touches left little behind in the way of natural cover.

"I see your point."

"You'll be okay," Pug said. "If anyone comes along, stand on one leg and keep really still. They'll think you're a lawn ornament."

"Shouldn't we at least go over to the far side of the tower and try to get out of sight a little bit?"

"But then we might miss Zirac when he comes back," Pug said. "He might get inside the tower before we can do anything about it. I have a better idea."

Hand outstretched, Pug walked up to the tower door.

"You don't want to do that," Thundar warned. "Wizards put spells on their property. You'll likely turn into a rat or a skunk or an eagle if you so much as lay a finger on that door latch."

"But look, it's already open." Pug nudged the door slightly ajar.

Thundar laughed. "Zirac forgot to shut the door to his tower? Was he drunk?"

"He forgot to lock it anyway. The door opened like nothing when I pushed on it."

"Maybe the fumes from the bat guano on the roof are getting to him at last."

Pug ducked his head inside the doorway. "Now that we're here, we should take a look around."

Thundar nodded. "Zirac would want it that way. I've never been inside a sorcerer's tower. What do you see?"

"It's fairly dark, but there's a light shining down from the window upstairs."

"Any treasure?" Thundar stepped closer to the door. "Gold bullion and the like?"

"No, nothing like that. It's just regular stuff."

Thundar stretched out his neck and peered through the open doorway. Cooking vessels, sacks of bulk foodstuffs, barrels of cooking oil, and other food items virtually filled the lower chamber of the tower, as if the mage were stocking up to withstand a siege. A spiral staircase led upward through the shadows.

Without a word of warning, Pug trotted across the chamber and mounted the stairs. He hopped over two and three steps at a time, ascending halfway up the stairwell before reversing course and speeding back down at an even greater rate. On his heels came a waif, a horror of otherworldly origin, incorruptible, immortal, and death to any mortal foolish enough to come into contact with it. This particular example of corrupted sorcery had been reanimated in the form of a giant human eyeball, but regardless of their shape, all waifs shared the same general traits, among them an unbreakable loyalty to whatever mage held them in thrall, a ceaseless vigilance in protecting their assigned territory, and an impervious nature to weapons of nonmagical origin.

"Run, you cannot fight it," Thundar shouted.

Pug never had a chance. Thundar gritted his teeth as the waif closed over the servant boy from behind, a malevolent mist, evil and intelligent.

The waif disappeared with an audible pop, gone from sight in an instant. Vanished like a broken soap bubble. Thundar rubbed his eyes. The waif was really and truly disappeared. To add to his amazement, Pug appeared unhurt if slightly confused. Impossible.

"Are you unscathed?"

"Yes. What was that thing?"

"A magical guardian. It's the last thing you should have ever seen. Are you in possession of a spell to counter so powerful an adversary?"

Pug laughed. "Do I look like a magician? I'm not in possession of any spells. That thing didn't even touch me. Look, here comes another one."

Thundar watched in astonishment as a second waif floated down the staircase and descended over Pug—and vanished. In quick succession, a dozen more of the creatures emerged from the chamber above. Each encounter with Pug resulted in one less waif in the tower. Finally only the glow coming through the window above reached down to touch them.

"Pug, have you received any training in the Arts?"

Pug snorted. "I'm a servant. What need have I for training in magic?"

"Something isn't adding up," Thundar said. "Do you know what a magic damper is?"

Pug shook his head.

"The old songs speak of rare individuals," Thundar said. "Of humans who dissipated magic through their bodies in much the same way as a lightning rod protects a tall building during a storm. Magic did not affect these people. Even a trained magician might have had trouble fending off an attack by a waif, let alone by a score of them, but you did so with seemingly no effort at all. Have you ever noticed this effect before now?"

"No," Pug said. "Never. Well, there were those times when when I overheard Zirac's conversations because his silence spells didn't work, but that was a problem with the magic, and no doing of my own."

"How can you know? Are you certain the magic simply didn't affect you?"

Pug scratched his head. "I don't know anything for certain."

"The tower door," Thundar said. "It opened when you pushed on it. A magical lock would be as nothing to a magic damper."

"Who cares?" Pug said. "I want nothing to do with magic. What I do want is to climb this staircase and see what's on the top floor."

"Zirac would want it that way," Thundar agreed. "But just in case we meet any more magical surprises, maybe you should lead the way."

Chapter Forty

Zirac lashed the wagon team without mercy.

The wagon tilted precariously hurling around a corner, but he did not let up on the horses for a moment. The sole safe haven still remaining to him, his tower, stood empty and waiting and fully provisioned only a few blocks ahead.

"You're crazy, Zirac," Gwendolyn called from within the wagon. "Untie me and the Emperor might let you live yet."

"Quiet, my wife." Zirac laughed. "You shall learn your place, and do so very soon at that."

"The Emperor will never let you get away with this. He will send all of his forces against you."

"My tower is secure," Zirac announced. "Strong enough to hold up until my ogre armies get here. A siege engine would knock the tower down sure enough, but the Emperor would never give the order to do so with his daughter still inside. A coalition of wizards on direct order from the Emperor might overwhelm my own defenses, but it'll never happen. Mages are notorious for fighting among each other."

"I despise you, Zirac."

Zirac waved his hand. "I couldn't care less. Many royal marriages are founded on a basis of mutual dislike. You shall come to love me, or you shall not, but it's really irrelevant. We will marry, the waif can perform the ceremony, and we shall start a family. I will sit on the throne one day, either through my marriage to you or by the brute force of my ogres. Nothing can stop me now."

"You're a monster."

"You should count your blessings. Any woman with a brain would be thrilled, indeed honored, to serve a man such as myself."

Zirac chuckled at his wit, his every sense awash with the ecstasy of victory. The carriage careened around the last corner before the tower.

The laughter died in his throat.

A veritable army of the Emperor's forces surrounded his tower. Armed for war with sword and pike and bow, they stood in ranks twenty deep.

"Mage," called a familiar voice.

Zirac spotted the Emperor seated on a horse surrounded by guards. Atop a second steed, the harlot, Katja, smirked like a rabid weasel.

"The game is over, Zirac," the Emperor shouted. "This woman alerted us to the army of ogres hiding in the mountains. Your friends were wiped out. They're not coming. Not now. Not ever."

Zirac hopped to the ground and flung open the carriage door. A flick of his dagger sliced away the cords restraining Gwendolyn's feet. He held the blade against her throat and dragged her outside.

"Get back or I'll cut her," he yelled. "Get back."

Hundreds of unsmiling soldiers drew their swords simultaneously, filling the air with a metallic rasp.

"I mean it. I'll bleed her like a pig."

"Halt," called the Emperor. "Let the mage pass. His type has no compunction against doing harm to a defenseless woman."

"It's over, Zirac," Gwendolyn said. "Throw yourself on my father's mercy. He is forgiving."

"Shut up." Zirac hustled his future bride toward the tower, the blade pressed hard against her windpipe. "I can hold out for years with the supplies stashed inside. Ogres or not, after a couple of our children arrive, your idiot father will have no choice but to recognize them as his heirs and myself as ruler of the Empire."

"You're mad."

"Move," Zirac ordered.

The door to the tower, and safety, stood only a few paces ahead.

"What happened here?" Thundar suppressed a shiver.

Broken glass and splintered furniture littered the topmost room of the tower. Dead creatures of strange and bestial types oozed gelatin and bodily fluids upon the floor. Blood stains covered entire sections of the walls. Several human skulls mounted atop a large wooden desk had been crushed flat.

Voices shouted from outside. Pug walked up the window. He dropped into a crouch.

"They must have seen us."

"Who?"

Pug pointed. "Look out there and see for yourself."

Thundar crept up to the windowsill and peered out.

"Soldiers? What are they doing here? They didn't come for us, else they'd be calling for us to come out. And there's the Emperor on a horse. What's going on?"

A carriage pulled by four horses came hurling down the street. Zirac sat atop the driver's seat. The carriage came to a stop. The Emperor shouted. Zirac shouted back. Thundar was unable to make out either man's words, but the tone of the conversation was openly hostile. Zirac opened the carriage door and . . .

"Hey," Thundar said. "Zirac is holding the Lady Gwendolyn prisoner. And he has a dagger against her neck."

Pug rushed up to the window.

Thundar watched in horror as the mage dragged the blonde woman across the castle grounds. The knife at her neck flashed as if in warning. Scores of soldiers drew their swords but none so much as moved a hand to help the princess.

"We have to do something," Pug said.

"Right. But what?"

"If only I had a bow and knew how to use it."

Thundar glanced around the room, seeking a weapon, any weapon. He spotted an old cabinet pushed up against a wall. Made from oak, the bulky piece likely weighed a hundred pounds or more.

"Can we move that cabinet up to the window and drop it on top of Zirac?"

"It's pretty big. But we can try."

Pug grunted and moaned pushing the cabinet across the floor.

"It's heavy."

"Just a little more," Thundar said. "Good. Now tilt the top forward so it goes out the window."

"What if it lands on the Lady Gwendolyn?"

Thundar peeked out the window: the mage was nearly at the tower door.

"Hurry! Zirac is going to make it inside." Thundar reached up and yanked on the top of the cabinet just as Pug's shoulder slammed against the backside. The cabinet shifted.

Thundar lost his balance and fell out the window.

Gerald gnashed his teeth.

Zirac held the Lady Gwendolyn in front of his body like a human shield, making it impossible to shoot the mage without first putting an arrow through the princess.

"Don't let him get inside the tower," called a soldier.

The royal archers held their bows taut.

"Do not let loose a single shaft unless you can do so without killing my daughter," the Emperor ordered. "On your lives."

Zirac screamed a stream of profanities. Gerald drew back his bowstring all the way to his cheek, desperate to find an opening. A wisp of movement in the window in the uppermost part of the tower caught his attention, a flash of motion, a blur of red scales that came plummeting to earth and smote Zirac directly atop the head and shoulders. The mage fell in a heap and did not move. The Lady Gwendolyn was left still standing. Unhurt.

Troops cheered wildly.

Chapter Forty-One

"You're a good man," the Emperor said. "I like the cut of your jib."

Thundar shuffled his feet atop the padded seat opposite the throne.

"Many thanks, Sire, but of course, I did not act alone."

"Nonsense, you'd have put a falcon to shame the way you swooped down out of the sky like that."

Thundar chuckled. "Just part of being a dragon."

"I thought maybe you had fallen out of the window," the Emperor continued. "But when you twisted around at the last moment and broke that mangy wizard's neck, now that was a sight to behold. Too bad about your wing. Will the bone heal properly?"

Thundar held out the appropriate appendage, heavily bandaged.

"The doctor isn't sure. He said that I might never fly again, master of the skies no more. Might as well be a death sentence for a dragon. My kind live to soar among the clouds."

"There, now," the Emperor said. "You just rest and eat and worry not about the future. If it turns out you can't fly again, there are plenty of diversions around the castle to help soften the blow. Enough to keep you happy for the rest of your life. Don't despair."

Thundar nodded. "I'll try."

Prince Gerald coughed into his hand. "As I was saying, the guard station atop the Southern Pass must be activated as soon as possible. It is folly to abandon the primary defenses of the Empire."

"Of course," the Emperor said. "I only ordered the station closed on Zirac's suggestion, unaware that I was being drugged at the time. A garrison is on the march to take control of the pass even at this moment."

Thundar glanced around the throne room. Royals in rich dress made up the majority of the party guests. Rogan and Parrot presented a contrast to the highborn elites in their plain, unwashed tunics.

The Lady Gwendolyn sat positioned between the throne and her future husband. A smile never left her face. A deep scratch along the side of her neck appeared the sole physical damage from her abduction by Zirac. Every few seconds, she flashed Gerald a stare of seductive approval, though the prince seemed as oblivious to her flirtations as ever.

"That woman who alerted us to the ogres," the Emperor said. "The one that poisoned the horse. She proved to be a loyal subject in the end and undoubtedly saved many lives. I'll bestow a duchy on her and the estates that go along with it. And the servant, Pug, for his helping save Gwendolyn's life, why, he'll be giving orders from now on instead of taking them at his new estate."

"You are kind, Sire," Thundar said.

The Emperor sat back in his throne. "The old magician's tower will be razed and a monument erected in its place. I see a bronze statue of the hero of the realm in its place, Thundar, captured in bronze, sweeping down from the skies to smite his enemies."

"Sire," Thundar managed. "You do me too much honor. Chronicler, did you hear the Emperor's words?"

"Yes, yes." Parrot scrawled on a scroll.

"A big statue?" Thundar asked.

The Emperor nodded. "Huge."

A servant bowed low before the throne. "Begging his majesty's pardon, but the doctor wishes another look at the young dragon's injured wing so as to ensure that infection does not set in."

"You'd better go," the Emperor said. "We don't want bad blood keeping you down."

"I'll take him." Gerald stood. "I wish to stretch my legs."

Gerald's shoulder seemed somehow narrower than Thundar remembered, but he refrained from commenting on the odd phenomena. Guards stood at attention as Gerald departed the throne room. The prince's booted feet echoed in the long, empty corridor leading to the offices of the court doctor.

"Can you imagine what might have happened?" Gerald said. "If the Lady Gwendolyn had been slain, there would have been no successor to the throne, which might well have led to civil war. The royal families would have battled it out between each other for control, and the ogre invasions would have destroyed whoever was left. You might have just saved the Empire."

Thundar nodded. "All this extra weight I strategically gained sure came in handy. But what now? Do you anticipate trouble with the royals? Will they accept that one of their own was not chosen as the consort of the princess?"

Gerald shrugged. "If anyone makes too much noise about that or any other issue, I'll have the Emperor threaten to move royal court permanently to Bogwood. When the Emperor grudgingly relents on the issue and agrees to keep the court in Empire City, the nobles will be so relieved that they'll agree to anything in its place."

"You shall miss North Bogsonia," Thundar said.

Gerald laughed, a strange light in his eyes. "Why do you say that?"

"Because you said so. You said so many times. That you do not like Empire City, and that you wished to be on your way back to Bogwood. But as part of the royal family, you will live the rest of your life in Empire City." Thundar shook his head.

"It is my destiny to become Emperor. Didn't you know?"

Thundar nearly fell from his perch.

"But . . . you always said that you didn't even want to be a king."

"King of North Bogsonia, no, but ruler of the Empire? Who wouldn't want that throne?" Gerald smiled. "I have known since I was a child that one day I would be Emperor. It is what I was born to do."

"Oh," Thundar said. "Did you always want the Lady Gwendolyn as well, even though you said you didn't?"

"Of course. Misdirection is an important part of being an effective leader. Never let them see your hand. A woman like Gwendolyn requires a special handling, else you end up like Rogan. And I certainly wasn't going to get anywhere with her slobbering all over her footsteps like everybody else had."

Thundar laughed so hard that a spurt of fire erupted from his nostrils.

"Well, I'll be an eagle. Tell me more."

End